The Midnight Pony

and other stories

Amanda Wills

ISBN: 1539143856
ISBN-13: 978-1539143857

For Adrian, Oliver and Thomas.

The Midnight Pony

1
Abracadabra

Ella Morgan narrowed her eyes and watched the magician pluck a playing card from behind Molly's left ear.

"It's the five of hearts!" gasped her best friend, wide-eyed. "But that's not possible!"

"That's magic," said the magician, waving his white-gloved hand and bowing theatrically. He smiled as the audience clapped and cheered. Ella sat on her hands in silence and wondered how anyone could have been fooled by such trickery.

"He had the card up his sleeve the whole time," she muttered to her best friend as they followed Molly's parents out of the theatre.

Molly's brow knotted in confusion. "It was behind my ear. You saw him take it!"

"I saw him poke it up his sleeve when everyone was watching the handkerchief he was waving around. There's no such thing as magic. If there was, I'd pull a pony out of my dad's old woolly hat tonight," Ella grinned. A delicious thought struck her. "Or make myself disappear so I didn't have to go to Aunt Rowan's."

Working out how the magician had pulled off his tricks had at least stopped her thinking about the morning.

"I think your Aunt Rowan is cool," said Molly. "Think how exciting it's going to be, staying in her amazing writer's garret perched on the cliffs."

Ella snorted. "She's not cool, she's weird. And the house isn't amazing, it's cold and draughty. I've got to spend my ninth birthday there, Molly. And there isn't a pony in miles. It's going to be terrible."

Cool. That wasn't a word Ella associated with

Aunt Rowan. Her dad's sister was tall and thin and slightly stooped from all the years she'd spent sitting at her typewriter, writing the long and complicated children's fantasy books that had made her fame if not her fortune.

She'd given her latest novel to Ella for her eighth birthday. Set in a galaxy far, far away, the book was about five centimetres thick and had taken Aunt Rowan five years to write. Ella had bravely ploughed through the first couple of chapters and then admitted defeat. The characters' names all sounded the same and they all spoke strangely. But the book came in very handy as a door stop.

Aunt Rowan wore long, flowing clothes in the colours of jewels. Small, round, wire-rimmed glasses sat on the end of her aquiline nose. Her hair was the same dark red as Ella's, but while Ella wore hers loose around her shoulders, Aunt Rowan's was swept up into a complicated knot at the top of her head. They also shared the same green eyes. "The colour of the ocean on a stormy night," her dad often said fondly.

Molly had been uncharacteristically quiet the

one and only time she'd met Aunt Rowan. Afterwards she had whispered to Ella, "Do you know what she reminds me of?"

Shaking her head, Ella had ventured, "A complete and utter eccentric?"

"No!" Molly had glanced over her shoulder to check no-one was listening. "She reminds me of a *witch*."

Seeing the puzzled expression on her best friend's face, Molly had said hastily, "Not an *evil* witch. A white witch. One of the nice, kindly ones you get in children's storybooks."

Ella had sighed. "Your imagination has been working overtime again. Aunt Rowan isn't a witch. She's just an *aunt*."

2

Goodbye Rocky

Ella stood on the sandy beach, her packed bag at her feet, and stared out to sea. Waves tumbled over themselves in their race to the shore.

"I thought we were going to Aunt Rowan's," she said, confused.

"Change of plan," said a voice she didn't recognise. Ella spun around. The magician was standing a few feet away, a white rabbit tucked under one arm. His eyes were as hard as flint. "You can't go. You don't believe in magic." He took a step towards Ella and she backed into the surf.

"So where do I go?" she cried.

He raised his hand and pointed to the ocean. Ella turned and ran, almost falling over her own feet in her hurry to get away. She plunged into the sea. The water was bitingly cold. She didn't notice the swell of a huge wave as it rolled towards her with the power of a high-speed train.

The wave tore through her, knocking the air from her lungs. She kicked her legs, gasping for breath. The surging sea foamed around her. White horses, Ella thought hazily. Can they save me?

But the white horses paid no attention to her as they danced in the surf. Little by little Ella felt her strength slip away. It became harder and harder to stay afloat. Her eyes fluttered shut.

Suddenly a shrill whinny pierced the air. Ella looked around her in panic. Had the white horses finally seen her? Her eyes widened. There, just ahead of her, a pony was struggling to stay afloat in the wild sea. His nostrils were flared and his eyes were rolling with terror. Ella felt strength return to her limbs and she struck out towards him. She could save him, she knew she could.

He was almost within reach when another wave crashed in, pulling him under. Ella trod water, desperately seeking the pony. But he was gone. She threw back her head and howled.

"There, there." Ella felt the cool touch of her mum's hand on her forehead. She opened her eyes. Under the glow of her bedside light her mum's face was full of concern.

"I was in the sea," Ella cried. "There was a pony -"

"It's OK," soothed her mum, stroking her cheek. "You're safe. There's no sea and no pony. It was just a bad dream."

Ella pulled her duvet under her chin. "It felt real," she said hollowly.

Ella pedalled furiously through the sleepy village, the dream still vivid in her mind. It was early, the sun was still low in the sky and the butchers and greengrocers shops were closed and shuttered. The only sign of life came from the bakery, where Mrs Johnson was piling freshly-baked rolls in the window. The smell made Ella's stomach rumble loudly. Mrs Johnson poked her head out.

"You're an early bird," she said.

Ella squeezed her brakes and her bike skidded to a halt. "I'm going to say goodbye to the ponies."

"I heard your mum and dad were off again," said Mrs Johnson, wiping her hands on her apron. "It's Arctic foxes this time, isn't it?"

Ella's parents were marine biologists and were due to fly off to an Arctic research station that evening. She nodded.

"Well, you have a good time at your Aunt Rowan's," said the shopkeeper, reaching into the window for a roll which she offered Ella, who took it gratefully.

"I don't suppose I will. But thanks anyway Mrs Johnson."

Soon Ella had left the village and turned down the bumpy lane to the stables. The sign on the gate said Ivyleaf Equestrian Centre, which made it sound very grand. It had been once, but not these days. The owner, Mrs Bee, had for a time been a famous dressage rider. But that was fifty years ago and Mrs Bee was now in her eighties. Still ramrod straight and with a voice as piercing as a startled seagull, she had swapped her string of top flight dressage horses for paying liveries. They included Molly's pony Henry, a sturdy skewbald with long feathers and a mischievous glint in his eye.

These days Mrs Bee only had two horses of her own, a bright bay draft horse called Oscar, and Rocky, the elderly Fjord horse Ella had learnt to ride on.

Ella jumped off her bike and flung it on the grass. Rocky was dozing under his favourite apple tree but when he heard her call he opened one eye and whickered. She tore up a handful of grass and vaulted the gate into his field.

"Oh Rocky, I'm going to miss you!" she cried, throwing her arms around his light dun neck.

Rocky nuzzled her pockets, hoping for another treat. Ella ran her hands through his bristly mane and felt a wave of sadness wash over her. Mrs Bee had announced the previous week that she would be retiring Rocky in the summer and Ella's weekly lessons would have to stop. It was May now, so she only had a few precious weeks left riding the little dun gelding.

"And I'm wasting one of them at Aunt Rowan's," she moaned. "It's not fair."

The drive to Aunt Rowan's was long and windy, and Ella stared out of the window trying not to feel carsick. Fields of wheat and corn gave way to rocky terrain as they neared The Lookout, the house her dad and Aunt Rowan had grown up in.

"Did I tell you about the time Rowan and I got cut off by the tide and had to climb the cliffs to safety?" her dad asked.

"Yes," said Ella, who had heard the story a hundred times.

"Promise me you won't go near the cliffs, Ella," her mum said in a worried voice.

"I promise."

The road narrowed and began to climb steadily, following the jagged contours of the cliffs. Ella wound down her window and breathed deeply. She could taste the salt in the air. They were almost there.

"Do you remember the first time we came?" said her dad as he pulled into a layby in the shadow of the cliffs. "You thought Rowan must live in a cave."

"What else was I supposed to think?" said Ella. Most people lived on normal streets and parked right outside their homes. Not Aunt Rowan. Visitors to The Lookout had to climb precisely two hundred and thirty two steps cut into the rock face to reach the house that had been built by Ella's great, great grandfather over a hundred years ago.

By the time they'd reached the rickety gate at the top of the steps they were all out of breath. Ella leant on the gate and gazed at the house. The Lookout always reminded her of a ship in a children's adventure book. At the prow was an octagonal tower with windows looking out to sea. At the very top of the tower was Aunt Rowan's study. Not that Ella had ever been allowed inside. The room was strictly out of bounds when her aunt was writing, which was most of the time.

Under the higgledy-piggledy roof line the weather-boarded walls, bleached silver in the sun, were cracked and warped. Ivy had grown unchecked across windows, cutting out the light. The seaweed-green paint on the front door was flaking. The house looked even more ramshackle than Ella remembered.

She took a deep breath and tugged on the rusty doorbell.

3

The Lookout

The door creaked and swung open. Aunt Rowan stepped out, her arms outstretched.

"You're here!" she cried. "We've been watching out for you, haven't we Tabitha?"

At the sound of her name, Aunt Rowan's Siamese cat shot out of the house. Ella knelt on the floor and called softly, wondering if Tabitha remembered her. The cat scampered over and held up her chin to be tickled.

Aunt Rowan smiled. "Tabitha has been looking forward to you coming to stay, Ella."

Ella followed her parents and aunt into the kitchen, which was just as she remembered -

large, cluttered and smelling of the wild herbs
Aunt Rowan dried in bunches above her
blackened range. Her aunt busied herself
making coffee while Ella and her parents sat
down at the kitchen table.

Her dad looked around him and sighed
contentedly. "It's good to be home. I just wish
we could stay longer."

"When do you have to leave?" Aunt Rowan
asked.

Ella's mum checked her watch. "In half an
hour. Otherwise we won't make the flight."

"I still can't believe you're missing my
birthday," Ella said indignantly.

"I know, sweetheart, and I'm sorry. You can
have your present when we're home." She
gave Ella's hand a squeeze and smiled. "We'll
be back before you know it."

Ella was silent. Seven whole days seemed
like forever. And what would she do with
herself while Aunt Rowan was locked away in
her study writing?

As if reading her thoughts, Aunt Rowan
said, "A woman with a son about Ella's age is
renting Flint Cottage for the summer. He's

called Axel." She peered down her long nose at Ella. "You'll have someone to play with while I'm working."

"When's the new book due out?" her dad asked and Ella tuned out as the talk drifted from Aunt Rowan's writing to the research her parents would be carrying out in the Arctic. She wondered if Molly was at the stables and felt a dart of homesickness as she pictured Henry and Rocky grazing side by side in their paddock.

The sound of chairs scraping on the flagstone floor jolted Ella out of her daydream. Ella and her aunt watched her parents disappear down the two hundred and thirty two steps to the road below.

"And then there were two," said Aunt Rowan brightly. "Or three, if you count Tabitha," she added, as the Siamese wound herself around Ella's legs. "Shall we show you where you'll be sleeping?"

Ella followed Aunt Rowan up the sweeping mahogany staircase and along a creaky corridor to a room at the front of the house.

"I normally sleep in the old nursery," said

Ella, surprised.

"I thought it was time you had a bigger bedroom," said her aunt.

She opened the door to reveal a large room with wood panelled walls and a four poster bed with velvet drapes the colour of sapphires. It was the only piece of furniture on show. Everything else was hidden beneath dust sheets. Ella dumped her rucksack on the floor and edged over to the window. Expecting to see the small band of lawn that circled the house she was surprised. Beneath her was the ocean.

"You're in the tower room, underneath my study. I think you'll like it here," said Aunt Rowan, joining Ella by the window. They watched the waves together until Aunt Rowan began to fidget.

"Will you be alright here for a little while?" she asked. "I must get some work done before supper."

Ella nodded. "It'll give me a chance to unpack."

The minute Aunt Rowan had left the room Ella set to work, tugging at the dust sheets to reveal the furniture underneath. A chest of drawers that was as tall as she was. A mahogany dressing table with a large, oval mirror that was crackled with age. Two matching bedside tables.

The last dust sheet hid a large grandfather clock with a sun and moon etched onto its face. It was six o'clock. Ella unzipped her case, threw her clothes into drawers and collapsed, exhausted, on the four poster bed.

She stared at the wall opposite her. A brass wall light hung above an empty picture hook. She walked over and inspected the wallpaper beneath the light. It was much darker than the rest of the wall. Aunt Rowan must have taken down a painting before she arrived. But why? Ella glanced around. There were no other paintings in the room. Perhaps it was a portrait of one of their fiercer-looking ancestors and she was worried it would give Ella nightmares.

Ella yawned. She would ask Aunt Rowan about the mysterious painting later. But first she would have a catnap. She wriggled under the duvet. The tick tock, tick tock of the old grandfather clock was hypnotic. In seconds she was fast asleep.

4

Tuna and Tinned Tomatoes

The melodic chime of the grandfather clock roused Ella from her slumber. Groggily, she counted the chimes. One, two, three, four, five, six, seven, eight.... Eight o'clock? Surely it couldn't be that late? Worried she'd missed supper, Ella jumped out of bed and ran down the stairs two at a time. She burst into the kitchen, full of apologies. But the kitchen was empty.

Ella trailed through the house, peering into each room in search of her aunt. Eventually she came to the study. The door was slightly ajar. Through the gap Ella could see Aunt Rowan sitting at a huge oak desk in the window, her chin cupped in her hands as she stared out to sea, lost in thought. In front of her was an old-fashioned typewriter. Next to it, Tabitha lay sprawled on an open notebook. On the floor by her aunt's feet was a bin overflowing with scrunched up sheets of typewritten paper.

Ella coughed politely. "I'm sorry I slept through supper, Aunt Rowan. Maybe I could have some cheese and crackers?"

Aunt Rowan turned and stared at her niece. "Supper?" she said, her face bemused. "Is it that time already?"

"It's a quarter past eight," said Ella.

Aunt Rowan's eyebrows shot up. "So it is! You must be ravenous." She pulled a sheet of paper from the typewriter, screwed it into a ball and flung it in the bin. "Writers' block. It's an author's worst enemy," she told Ella.

In the kitchen Aunt Rowan opened the larder to reveal shelves stacked high with tins and jars. "I'm not much of a cook, I'm afraid. I generally open a couple of the closest tins. It makes for some strange meals, but no-one could say I wasn't adventurous." She

inspected two tins inches from her nose.
"Tuna and tinned tomatoes. Will that do?"

Privately Ella thought it sounded disgusting,
but she was so hungry she would try anything.

"It might be nicer if we heat it up," she
suggested.

"Why didn't I think of that?"

Piled on toast, the tuna and tomato mixture
tasted much better than it sounded, and Ella
wolfed hers down in minutes.

"Your dad tells me you've been learning to
ride," said Aunt Rowan. "Do you like
ponies?"

Ella nodded. "I love them. I've been having
lessons every Saturday. I've just learned to
canter without stirrups."

"I'm impressed," said Aunt Rowan. "And
what pony do you ride?"

"Rocky. He's a Fjord horse. Do you know
what they look like?"

It was Aunt Rowan's turn to nod. "They're
the butterscotch-coloured ones with the spiky
black and white manes, aren't they?"

Ella giggled. "They're called dun, not
butterscotch, although that sounds much

nicer." Her face clouded over. "But Rocky's retiring this summer."

"So there'll be no pony for you to ride?" Her aunt was sympathetic.

Ella shook her head. "My best friend Molly has promised that I can ride her pony, Henry. He's a skewbald. That's brown and white," Ella added. "It's really kind of her, but it's not the same as having Rocky. I'm the only one who rides him these days, so I can sort of pretend he's mine, even though he isn't really."

"Maybe your mum and dad will buy you your own pony?"

Ella met her aunt's kindly gaze. "Dad says they're too expensive."

"You can't put a price on someone's dreams," said Aunt Rowan.

Ella didn't really understand what she meant, but she nodded anyway and stifled a yawn. Despite her nap she still felt sleepy.

"It's all that sea air," said Aunt Rowan. "Why don't you get an early night? I'll introduce you to Axel in the morning."

"Is that the boy who's staying in Flint

Cottage?" Ella asked.

Aunt Rowan nodded.

"What's he like?"

Aunt Rowan considered this. "Puffins," she said finally.

Ella scrunched up her face in confusion, and then giggled. "I mean what is he like, not what does he like," she said.

"Ah, of course, how silly of me," her aunt smiled. "You'll find out tomorrow, won't you?"

5
Alex

After a deep, dreamless sleep Ella woke the next morning to the sound of waves crashing onto the rocks below her window. She dressed and ran downstairs. Aunt Rowan was clattering about in the larder and poked her head around the door when she heard Ella arrive.

"Are pickled gherkins and meatballs OK for breakfast?"

"I don't suppose there's any porridge?" Ella asked hopefully.

Aunt Rowan ducked back into the larder and reappeared with a box of porridge. "Probably best not to check the best before date, but oats don't really go off, do they?"

Fortunately Ella wasn't a fussy child. "I'm sure they'll be fine."

As she was drizzling honey over her porridge there was a knock at the door.

"That'll be Axel with the eggs," said Aunt Rowan. "Come in, Axel, the door's open."

A dark-haired boy burst into the kitchen, an egg box in his hands. Ella guessed he was probably about eleven. "Mum sent me over with these." The boy looked Ella up and down. "You must be Rowan's niece. I'm Alex."

"But Aunt Rowan called you Axel," said Ella.

"I know. She gets the letters the wrong way round. It's an easy mistake to make, even for someone who spends all day writing, apparently," grinned Alex. "Want me to show you around after breakfast? I know where the puffins nest. I can take you there if you want?"

Ella had to admit it sounded cool. She loved puffins, too. And no doubt Aunt Rowan would spend the day working on her latest doorstop of a book. She scraped the last of the porridge from her bowl. "Sure, why not?"

Ella followed Alex along a narrow path between thickets of gorse on the top of the cliffs. Seagulls wheeled and soared high above their heads, their cries carried away by the wind. It was warm for May, and she took off her jumper and tied it around her waist.

They followed the path for another ten minutes until Alex stopped. Holding a finger to his lips he pointed straight ahead. "Look at that headland," he whispered. "Can you see them?"

Ella squinted into the sun. On the rocky cliff face she could just make out a handful of puffins. With their strange bobbing gait, black and white feathers and distinctive orange beaks they reminded her of penguins.

"We're a bit too early in the season. Come June there will be thousands of them nesting here. Sometimes I bring my watercolours and sketchbook and sit and watch them for hours," said Alex.

"Don't you ever get bored here?" Ella asked.

Alex looked at her as if she was mad. "With all this on the doorstep?" He waved his hands over the bleak, rocky cliffs and the pounding sea below. "Are you kidding? There's so much to do. It's a magical place, can't you feel it?"

Ella shook her head. "There's no such thing as magic."

Alex chuckled. "If that's what you want to believe. Come on, we'd better head home."

Ella came down to breakfast the next day to find a handful of cards and two presents on the kitchen table.

"You remembered my birthday!"

Aunt Rowan's eyes twinkled. "I may not remember mealtimes or people's names, but I never forget your birthday, Ella. How could I when it's the same day as mine?"

"I never knew that," said Ella.

"It's best to try to forget birthdays when you're my age," said her aunt.

Ella couldn't imagine a time when she'd ever want to forget her birthday. She looked at her pile of presents and then at the empty space in front of Aunt Rowan.

"You haven't got anything."

"I don't mind. It's more fun to give than to receive."

Ella raised her eyebrows. Only a grown up could say something so strange.

"This one's from your mum and dad," said Aunt Rowan, handing Ella a parcel wrapped in glittery purple and silver paper. "They told me to tell you your main present will be waiting for you at home."

Ella tore the wrapping paper open to reveal a pair of riding gloves and an encyclopaedia on riding and pony care. "Cool," she said, trying on the gloves for size. They fitted perfectly.

"This one's from Axel. He dropped it by earlier."

"Alex," Ella corrected her. "I wonder how he knew it was my birthday." She took the flat, square parcel wrapped in brown paper and tied with string. Inside was a watercolour painting of a pair of puffins, standing on the cliffs looking out to sea.

"It's lovely," she said.

Aunt Rowan reached behind her and took a

large rectangular present from the dresser.

"I was going to give you one of my books, but a little bird tells me you use the last one I gave you as a doorstop."

Ella felt her cheeks redden.

"It's quite alright, Ella dear," said Aunt Rowan. "Fantasy books set in outer space aren't for everyone. Even I find them hard going at times, and I write them. No. Now you're nine I thought it was high time I gave you *this*."

6

Birthday Girl

Ella stared at the gift-wrapped present. She felt a fizz of excitement. What could it be? A jigsaw? A Lego set? She gave it a shake, but there was no answering rattle. Perhaps it was a book? But no, it was way too big for that.

Ella carefully tore open a corner and glanced up at her aunt. She was watching her intently, a smile playing on her lips. Unable to wait any longer, Ella ripped open the paper. Her hand flew to her mouth.

Inside the layers of paper was a painting of the most beautiful palomino pony Ella had ever seen, standing under a gnarled oak tree in front of a cascading waterfall. It was dark in the painting, and the night sky twinkled with stars. High above the waterfall a full moon shone brightly.

The pony's coat was the colour of honey and his mane and tail were as white as newly-fallen snow. He had one white sock on his near foreleg and a blaze on his face the shape of a bolt of lightning. But it was his eyes that melted Ella's heart. They were deep pools of chocolate brown and they gazed straight at her.

Ella was utterly entranced.

"This is a very special painting. I hope you like it," said Aunt Rowan.

"Like it? I love it! Thank you so much," Ella flung her arms around her aunt, who patted her back awkwardly.

"Where did you buy it?" asked Ella, thinking that the nearest art gallery must be at least fifty miles away.

"I didn't. It's a family heirloom."

"What does that mean?"

"It has been passed down the women of the Morgan family for generations."

"You mean it used to be yours?"

Aunt Rowan nodded. "And it was your grandmother's before that. You've inherited the painting from your ancestors, just as you inherited your red hair."

Over the years Ella had often wished she had blonde hair like Molly. Suddenly, red hair didn't seem so bad. Not if it meant the painting was hers. She studied it again, noticing a tiny oblong plaque cut into the frame.

"The Midnight Pony, by Agnes Morgan," she read. "Is she one of my ancestors?"

Aunt Rowan smiled. "She was your great, great grandmother."

"Was it a portrait? I mean, was this a real pony or did she paint him from her imagination?" Ella asked, tracing the palomino's lightning-shaped blaze with her finger.

"Who can say what's real and what isn't?" Aunt Rowan said mysteriously. "Where do you think we should hang it?"

"There's an empty picture hook on the wall in my bedroom. I meant to ask you about it and forgot," Ella said. "If we put it there I'll be able to see it from my bed."

She watched with satisfaction as Aunt Rowan hung the picture. It fitted in the space perfectly. Ella had a sneaking suspicion it had probably come from there in the first place. She imagined it hanging in her bedroom. It would look amazing.

"There is one condition attached to the painting, I'm afraid," said Aunt Rowan. "It must stay at The Lookout."

Ella's face fell. "I can't take it home?"

"I'm afraid not, Ella dear."

"Oh." Ella tried not to look too disappointed. "Why not?"

"Your great, great grandmother said it must never leave the house. It belongs here. One day you'll understand why."

Ella was puzzled. "What do you mean?"

Aunt Rowan ran her fingers along the window ledge. "I really must do some dusting," she said, half to herself.

Ella was about to quiz her further, but before she had a chance to open her mouth Aunt Rowan had disappeared along the hallway, muttering about feather dusters and beeswax.

"All things considered, it hasn't been a bad birthday at all," Ella told Tabitha as she turned on her bedside light and reached for her pyjamas.

The Siamese was sitting in front of the open window staring out to sea. It was true, Ella thought. After breakfast Aunt Rowan had declared it to be a No Writing Day and had packed a picnic of hardboiled eggs, tinned sardines and crackers. As they'd left the house they'd passed Alex, who was sitting on a rock with his watercolours and a sketchbook drawing one of his mum's hens as she pecked and scratched in the dirt.

Ella had thanked him for her puffin painting and Alex had asked if they wanted some company.

"The more the merrier," Aunt Rowan had said and they'd set off together, following the cliff path as it zigzagged around the headland. They'd climbed down some precarious steps to a tiny strip of pebbly beach where they'd eaten their lunch and paddled in the ice-cold sea.

When they'd finally arrived back at The Lookout, tired and windswept, Alex's mum Julie had appeared with a triple-tiered chocolate cake with nine candles on. Yes, all in all it had been a pretty good birthday.

Ella sat on the end of her bed and stared at her new painting. Under the creamy glow of the picture light the palomino pony stared back at her, his honey-coloured coat gleaming and his expression gentle and trusting. The painting was so lifelike Ella could almost feel the tickle of his whiskers on her hand, and hear the roar of the waterfall behind him.

Tabitha jumped on the bed, purring loudly. Ella closed the window and pulled the curtains. As she walked past the painting she kissed her fingers and touched the palomino's nose.

"Goodnight, Midnight Pony," she whispered. "Sweet dreams."

7

The Clock Strikes Midnight

Ella woke with a start to the sound of a clock chiming. Ding. It sounded faint, as if it was coming from the end of a very long tunnel. Ding. There it was again. She lifted her head and listened as the clock chimed ten more times. It was twelve o'clock. Midnight.

The chimes faded and Ella became aware of another noise - the sound of water crashing onto rocks. Like the sea but different. More like a waterfall.

Ella was puzzled. She was sure she'd closed her bedroom window. She squinted into the darkness, trying to see if the curtains were flapping in the breeze. Above her tiny pinpricks of light sparkled. Almost like stars, Ella thought. She rubbed her eyes and looked again. Yes, they definitely looked like stars. Perhaps Aunt Rowan had fixed a string of fairy lights around the four poster bed as an extra birthday surprise.

Ella sat up, all thoughts of sleep forgotten. She stared out of the window at the moon. It stared back at her, casting everything in a silvery light. She felt her tummy somersault. She had closed the window and pulled the curtains. So how come she could see the moon and stars?

Then several things happened at once. Ella went to fling off her duvet but instead felt soft blades of grass beneath her fingers. She scrambled to her feet and spun around. The four poster bed had disappeared. The grandfather clock, the tall chest of drawers and the bedside tables had all vanished. And an owl glided past, hooting softly as it landed on the branch of a gnarled old oak tree that stood where the door to her bedroom ought to have been.

The owl watched Ella, its amber eyes

unblinking, as she ran up to the tree and touched its trunk, expecting it to turn back into one of the oak bedposts. It didn't. She followed the sound of pounding water.

The sight of the waterfall took Ella's breath away. Moonlight turned the water silver as it tumbled down the rock face. She stared into the deep pool at the bottom and a solemn-faced girl with green eyes and dark red hair gazed back at her.

Ella turned away from her reflection, her heart thudding in her chest. She knew she was only dreaming, but it didn't matter. She was in her great, great grandmother's painting. And - somewhere - was the palomino pony she'd fallen in love with.

8
Blaze

He was watching her from behind the oak
tree, his chocolate brown eyes fixed on hers.
Ella called softly and he took a couple of steps
forwards. She bent down and pulled up a
handful of grass, offering it to him on her
outstretched hand. She clicked her tongue
encouragingly and he took another few steps
towards her.

"Don't be frightened, I won't hurt you. I
only want to say hello," Ella murmured. She
edged forwards, her hand still outstretched.
Soon she was just a couple of paces away
from the pony. She held her breath as he took
the last couple of steps to her. His whiskers

tickled her fingers as he nibbled the grass, just as she'd imagined they would.

Ella slowly reached up and rubbed his lightning-shaped blaze. He gave her a friendly nudge.

"Blaze," Ella said thoughtfully. "That's the perfect name for you. I'm Ella and I am very pleased to meet you. We have met already of course." She paused. "Sort of, anyway."

Blaze stood patiently while Ella picked more grass for him and wondered what he'd be like to ride. Once the thought was in her head she couldn't think of anything else.

"Would you mind?" she asked. He did seem very tame, and it was only a dream, after all, so nothing could go wrong. Ella spied a rock about the size of the mounting block at Ivyleaf and walked over to it, delighted when Blaze followed her. He stood obediently next to the rock while Ella climbed onto it. She leant over his back experimentally.

"How does this feel?" she asked him. The little palomino pony didn't flinch. Encouraged, Ella vaulted on as lightly as she could. Blaze tossed his head and his mane shimmered in the moonlight.

Ella had ridden Rocky bareback plenty of times and although Blaze wasn't as broad as the Fjord horse she sat astride him easily. She wound a hank of his long mane around one hand and ran her other hand down his neck. His golden coat was as soft as silk.

Are dream horses the same as real ones? Ella wondered. She squeezed her legs and Blaze walked on, following a narrow track through the trees that Ella hadn't noticed before. She squeezed again and he broke into a trot. She clicked her tongue and he began to canter, his neck arched proudly. He had the floatiest of paces. It was like riding a cloud.

Shafts of moonlight pierced the trees and in the dappled light the girl and pony cantered on. Ella's hair and Blaze's tail streamed behind them like red and white ribbons. Blaze was as surefooted as a mountain goat and Ella had no fear that he would trip and fall. She glanced behind her, wondering if she would ever find her way back to the waterfall. Then she remembered that it didn't matter. All she had to do was wake up and she'd be back in her bedroom at The Lookout, staring at Blaze in a painting.

They raced on through the trees, startling a pair of roe deer, before finally emerging in a wildflower meadow so beautiful it took Ella's breath away.

"Whoa," she said softly. Blaze flicked an ear back and broke into a walk. "And halt."

He did just as he was asked.

"Clever boy!" she said, laughing when he turned his head and nibbled the hem of her pyjama bottoms.

She slid off and wrapped her arms around his neck. "That was the best ride of my life," she mumbled into his mane. "Thank you."

Ella sat cross-legged on the grass and watched Blaze graze until the moon sank in the sky and the first pink rays of dawn appeared on the horizon. She sighed. It had been a perfect dream and she didn't want it to end. Blaze wandered over and blew softly into her hair. Ella smiled through the tears that were trickling down her cheeks.

"I love you, Midnight Pony," she said quietly. "I wish you could be mine."

9
Only a Dream

A sliver of light crept through a crack in the curtains, dragging Ella from sleep. She yawned, blew her fringe out of her eyes and checked her alarm clock. Ten past nine. It was much later than she usually woke up. Remembering her wonderful dream, Ella forced her eyes shut and imagined she was back in the woodland glade with Blaze.

Screwing her face up in concentration, she pictured the gnarly old oak tree, the sound of the waterfall, the feel of Blaze's silky mane wound around her hand. But no matter how hard she tried to go back to sleep the shaft of sunlight danced on her closed eyelids and refused to let her slumber.

Sighing loudly, she sat up in bed and stared at the painting. Blaze gazed back at her, his brown eyes full of secrets, as if he knew about their adventure, too.

Ella shook her head. Who was she trying to kid? He was just a pony in a painting. He didn't exist outside her imagination. The dream may have felt real at the time. But that was all. It was just a dream. Just like the one she'd had the night before she'd arrived at Aunt Rowan's.

Ever since she could remember, Ella had preferred fact over fiction. While her friends' bedroom shelves were jammed with storybooks, Ella preferred books filled with facts. Most of all she loved facts about animals. Especially horses.

Remembering the book on riding and pony care her parents had given her for her birthday, Ella reached over to her bedside table. As she did, she noticed a wisp of cotton entwined around the fingers of her right hand. She would have ignored it, had it not been for the way the thread turned silver in the sunlight.

"That's funny," Ella murmured. For a moment she was back in the glade, watching the moonlight make Blaze's mane sparkle. She held each end of the thread between thumb and forefinger and studied it carefully, as if she was a scientist examining it under a microscope.

It wasn't cotton, Ella decided. It was too thick, too strong, too silky. And anyway, where would it have come from? Ella's pyjamas were red and the sheets and duvet cover were sapphire blue to match the drapes. If Ella didn't know better, she'd say it was a strand of hair. But even though she was ancient, Aunt Rowan's hair was still the same shade of dark red as Ella's own, and although Tabitha's hair was almost the right colour, it was far too short.

Without thinking, Ella glanced at the painting and her heart gave a funny little leap. And then she scolded herself. "Don't be ridiculous. Of course it's not. There must be a rational explanation."

Her bedroom door creaked open and her

aunt glided in and set a glass of orange juice, a bowl of tinned peaches and two ginger snap biscuits on her bedside table.

"I'm glad I'm not the only one who talks to myself," said Aunt Rowan, pulling the curtains open. "Sometimes it's the only way to have a decent conversation around here. Except when you're staying, of course," she smiled.

"I was talking to Tabitha," Ella lied, spying the Siamese asleep on top of the chest of drawers.

"I needed a break from the typewriter so I've brought you breakfast in bed." Aunt Rowan perched on the edge of the bed and studied Ella's face. "So, tell me, how did you sleep?"

Ella twiddled the length of hair around her fingers. If Aunt Rowan noticed, she didn't say anything. Ella was about to tell her aunt about the dream. But at the last minute something stopped her.

"Well?" prompted her aunt.

Ella nibbled on one of the ginger snap biscuits. "I slept well, thank-you."

"Sweet dreams?" pressed Aunt Rowan.

Ella hid behind her fringe. "Not especially,"

she shrugged. "Why?"

It was Aunt Rowan's turn to look uncomfortable. "No reason. I suppose I'd better get back to my desk. This book won't write itself." As she disappeared down the landing she called back to Ella. "I almost forgot. Axel popped by earlier. He wondered if you'd like to take a picnic to the waterfall."

10
The Waterfall

Ella's heart missed a beat. She must have misheard.

"Take a picnic where?" she croaked.

Silence.

She placed the strand of hair carefully between the pages of her new book, slithered out of bed and tore along the landing. But her aunt had already vanished up the narrow staircase that led to her study. Ella tiptoed up, holding onto the rope bannister and trying to avoid the creaky stairs. The door at the top was closed. A sign hanging from the doorknob said Do not disturb.

She won't mind, Ella thought, and went to

knock.

Her hand was poised mid-air when she heard the muffled clatter of Aunt Rowan's typewriter. Her aunt must have finally found a cure for her writer's block. And, judging by the frantic patter patter of the keys, she was on a roll.

Ella brought her hand back down by her side. If she interrupted Aunt Rowan while she was in the middle of writing she might disturb her train of thought and bring back the dreaded writer's block. The wastepaper bin would be overflowing again, Aunt Rowan would never finish the book and it would all be Ella's fault.

She spun on her heels and headed back down the corkscrew staircase. She would ask Alex if there was a waterfall. And if there was, she'd tell him she definitely wanted to go there.

Alex was packing sandwiches into a rucksack when Ella found him, ten minutes later.

"Rowan told you about the picnic?" he asked.

"She said something about a waterfall," said Ella breathlessly. "Is there one?"

Alex nodded. "It's a good two hour walk from here. But it's worth it, I promise." His brow furrowed. "It won't be too far for you, will it?"

Ella narrowed her eyes at him. "Of course it won't. I am nine, you know. I can walk for miles."

Alex held his hands up in surrender. "OK, OK. I just wanted to check, that's all." He slid his sketchbook and some charcoals into the rucksack and slung it over his shoulder. "Ready?"

Ella felt a tingle of excitement. "You bet!"

They set off in the opposite direction to the rocky cliff face where the puffins nested. Although the sky was the colour of cornflowers there was a chill wind and Ella was glad of her sweater.

The path was wide and sandy and headed steadily inland. After an hour and a half Ella's legs were beginning to tire and she was secretly relieved when Alex suggested they stop so he could sketch a clump of wood anemones. He handed her a bottle of water and she drank thirstily.

"What's the waterfall like?" she asked.

"You'll see it soon. We're nearly there."

"Is there a big oak tree near it?"

Alex looked at her in surprise. "I thought you said you hadn't been there before?"

Ella's heart was beating fast. "I haven't. I dreamt about a waterfall last night, and there was an oak tree there, too." And a beautiful palomino pony, she thought, but didn't say it.

"I often dream about places, but only when I've already been to them," said Alex, smudging a tiny charcoal anemone with the tip of his index finger. "Perhaps Rowan took you there when you were little."

That made perfect sense, thought Ella. Of course that's what must have happened.

But it still didn't explain the strand of hair.

Soon Ella heard the gurgle of running water and they reached a stream. It was wide and shallow and she could see tiny silver fish flitting about on the riverbed. She dipped her hand in. The water was icy cold.

"Not far now," said Alex.

They followed the stream as it wound its way through the rocky terrain. Ahead, the stream plunged into a forest. Ella couldn't wait any longer. She had to see the waterfall.

"Come on, let's run the last bit!" she cried, disappearing into the leafy canopy, Alex panting behind her. The sound of rushing water was becoming louder by the second. And then the trees petered out and Ella stopped in her tracks.

"What's up?" said Alex, almost colliding with her. She could barely hear him over the noise of the waterfall.

Ella stared at the gnarled old oak tree and the water cascading down the rocks behind it and her eyes shone with excitement.

If the waterfall and the oak tree were real, perhaps Blaze was too?

11

An Early Night

Picturing the painting of The Midnight Pony in her mind's eye, Ella worked out exactly where her great, great granny must have sat with her brushes and easel all those years ago.

She pointed to the spot. "We'll have our picnic here."

Alex passed her a ham and tomato roll. Ella scoured the wood, hoping to see a flash of gold between the trees. But the only thing she did see was a red squirrel flying through the branches like an acrobat on a trapeze.

"How easy is it to draw something from your imagination?" she asked Alex.

He chewed his roll thoughtfully. "It works

for some people. Otherwise there'd be no paintings of dragons or monsters or mermaids. But I prefer to draw from real life. Why?"

"Aunt Rowan gave me a painting for my birthday. It's by an artist called Agnes Morgan. She's one of my ancestors. It was painted in this glade, I'm certain of it. There's a pony in the picture, too."

"The Midnight Pony?" said Alex.

Ella gasped. "How do you know?"

"Rowan was wrapping the painting up when I popped the puffin picture over yesterday. Your ancestor was a very talented artist."

"She was," agreed Ella. "I'm just trying to work out if she painted the pony in the picture from her imagination or if he was really real."

"Why don't you ask Rowan? She might know."

"I will," said Ella. "The minute we get back."

But when Ella burst into the kitchen the first thing she saw was a scribbled note on the table.

Dearest Ella,

My writer's block has vanished and the words are finally flowing. I must, as the saying goes, make hay while the sun shines! I will be writing until the early hours. Julie will give you supper and I will see you at breakfast. I hope you don't mind.

Love from
Aunt Rowan

Ella sighed. She wouldn't be able to ask her aunt about Blaze tonight. She closed the back door behind her and headed for Flint Cottage.

Ella was so tired after their four hour walk that she could barely keep her eyes open as she sat at the table in Julie and Alex's tiny kitchen.

"Sorry," she said, every time she yawned.

"I think an early night is in order," said Julie. "Come on, I'll walk you up to The Lookout."

It was only seven o'clock but Ella was too tired to argue. She followed Julie up to the house and locked the door behind her. As she let herself into her bedroom she heard the reassuring tap tap of Aunt Rowan's typewriter above her. She stopped by the painting and kissed Blaze's nose.

"We went back to the glade today," she told him. "I wish you'd been there, too."

He looked at her with his gentle brown eyes. Even if he had been a real pony, Ella had done the maths. Agnes Morgan must have sat in the glade and painted the picture over one hundred years ago. According to Ella's treasured Guinness World Records book a grey Arab-Welsh cross gelding called Badger from the UK still held the title of the oldest horse in the world. And Badger had been fifty one when he died in 2004.

Ella was a practical girl and knew in her heart that Blaze didn't exist outside the ornate frame of Agnes's painting. All she could hope for was that he'd visit her again in her dreams.

Her shoulders sagging, she trudged over to the four poster, pulled back the drapes and climbed under the duvet. "Goodnight Blaze," Ella whispered. She turned on her side and in the blink of an eye was asleep.

If she'd stayed awake a second longer she

might have seen the little palomino pony paw the ground, impatient for another adventure.

But even if she had, she would have shaken her head and told herself she was letting her imagination run riot again.

Because there's no such thing as magic, is there?

12

The Daisy Chain

Once more Ella woke to the sound of the grandfather clock striking midnight. She could hear water, but was it the tumbling waterfall or the waves below her bedroom window? She couldn't tell. She lay still for a moment, her fingers crossed and her eyes pressed shut. Hoping against hope that when she opened them she would see Blaze waiting for her under the old oak tree and not the blue velvet drapes around her bed.

Ella slowly opened one eye, and then the other. A grin spread across her face. No drapes, no grandfather clock and no four walls. Instead, moonlight danced on the deep water of the pool at the foot of the waterfall and the leaves of the oak tree whispered and sighed in the wind. Jumping to her feet, she searched the glade for Blaze.

Her heart sang when he stepped out of the trees, his head held high and his eyes fixed on hers. She picked a handful of grass and offered it to him. This time he didn't hesitate.

"You remember me!" Ella laughed.

She pressed her cheek against his and he blew softly into her neck, sending a shiver of delight along her spine.

"I've missed you so much."

Blaze nudged Ella and stamped his foot.

"What are you trying to tell me?" she asked, scratching his ear. "Do you want more grass?"

He tossed his head impatiently.

"You want to go for another ride?"

Blaze whickered.

"I guess that's a yes." She grabbed a handful of mane and vaulted on. Remembering the hair she'd found wrapped around her fingers that morning she looked closely at his mane. The colour was a perfect match. So was the texture. Before she had a chance consider what it meant Blaze wheeled around and broke into a trot. Ella squeezed her legs and soon they were cantering through the trees on their way to the wildflower meadow.

Ella felt a wave of contentment wash over her. She sat easily, perfectly balanced on Blaze's back as if she'd been riding him all her life. As if they belonged together.

As if he was her destiny.

The grandfather clock chimed and Ella's eyes snapped open. It was morning. She was back in her bedroom and Blaze was back in his painting. She must have fallen asleep while she watched him graze among the wild flowers. She'd tried so hard to stay awake. She'd made daisy chains, she'd sung songs. She'd told Blaze about Molly, Henry and Rocky, about Ivyleaf and Mrs Bee.

"It's a bit shabby around the edges and Mrs Bee can be very strict. But I think you'd like it there," she'd said.

He'd stopped grazing to listen. Ella had thought how brilliant it would be to be able to ride with Molly and Henry. Imagine the fun the four of them would have. If only Blaze was a real, living, breathing pony, not a figment of her imagination.

Hearing Ella stir, Tabitha padded up the bed, purring.

"Hey, Tabs." Ella reached out to tickle the Siamese under her chin, exactly where she liked it best. As she did, something fell from her hand onto the rumpled sheet. Ella stared at it, her mouth open. She shook her head, thinking she must be wrong, and looked again.

Tiny white and yellow flowers, joined together by their stalks. Slightly squashed, the stalks bent and the petals mangled, but recognisable all the same.

A daisy chain.

13
Agnes Morgan

Ella found Aunt Rowan in the garden, sitting on a bench looking out to sea. Her aunt patted the seat beside her and Ella sat down, cross-legged, and began plaiting her hair absentmindedly.

"How's the writing going?" she said.

Aunt Rowan flexed her fingers. "I'm just taking a break. I've been up since four. But it's going well. Thank goodness."

They were silent for a while, watching the white horses as they surged and swirled in the gunmetal grey sea.

Aunt Rowan said, "You didn't track me down to ask me about my writing, did you?

What's up?" She gave a faint smile. "It's not my cooking, is it?"

Ella chewed her bottom lip. "No, it's not that. Although I'm not sure dumplings and anchovy paste actually go together."

"You never know, it could be the next big thing," laughed Aunt Rowan. Then, after a pause, she said, "You're not homesick, are you?"

"I thought I might be," Ella admitted. "But I haven't missed home at all. I like it here, despite your cooking," she grinned. "Actually, I wanted to talk to you about my painting."

"Ah," said Aunt Rowan. "I wondered if that was the case. What is it you want to know?"

"When you gave it to me I asked you if the pony in it was a real one, or if my great, great grandmother painted him from her imagination. You didn't really answer."

"I didn't, did I? As far as I know, he was real. According to family legend, Agnes was crazy about horses."

"I definitely inherited that gene," said Ella.

"Yes, she had a small herd of brood mares that she kept in the wildflower meadow past the waterfall. They kept her busy while your great, great grandfather was at sea." Aunt Rowan stood up. "Dear Ella, much as I love our chats I'm afraid my typewriter calls. Will you be able to amuse yourself again today?"

Ella nodded. "Alex is going to teach me how to draw a puffin. We're going back to the cliff where they nest."

But Aunt Rowan was wearing that faraway look on her face that meant she was back in her fictional world. Ella sat a while longer on the bench, gazing at the white horses and wondering about her great, great grandmother and what might have been.

Ella was helping Aunt Rowan dry up after their dinner - cod roe and tinned meatballs - when she faked a yawn and said casually, "I might head up to bed now."

Aunt Rowan glanced at the clock and raised her eyebrows. "It's only six o'clock. Are you unwell?"

"I'm fine. Just really, really tired. It must be all that sea air," said Ella, not meeting her aunt's eye.

"An early night's probably a good idea. Your mum and dad will be here just after breakfast."

Ella's face fell. "I forgot I was going home tomorrow."

"Time flies when you're having fun," said her aunt with a smile.

Ella kissed Aunt Rowan goodnight and raced up the stairs two at a time. By three minutes past six she had cleaned her teeth and changed into her pyjamas. By five past six she was tucked up in bed. At home she tried all sorts of delaying tactics to stay up as late as possible. Here it was the polar opposite. She couldn't wait to go to bed.

And tonight was important. Ella had a feeling that she wouldn't dream about Blaze once she was home and she wanted to make the most of her last night with him. She closed her eyes and let the sound of the waves lull her to sleep.

14
High Tide

Ella felt a waft of warm air on her neck. She opened her eyes. Blaze's face was a few centimetres from her own, his whiskers tickling her cheek. She propped herself up on her elbows and stared into his deep brown eyes.

"Hello you," she said.

The little palomino gelding whickered and gave her a nudge. Ella jumped to her feet. She was fizzing with energy, as if she could run a marathon or climb a mountain. She vaulted gracefully onto Blaze's back and grabbed a handful of his mane.

Under the pearly glow of the moon the glade had never looked more beautiful. The vivid green leaves of the old oak tree rustled in the breeze. The waterfall shimmered like a cloak of silver thread. The deep pool of water at its feet reflected a thousand twinkling stars. Blaze's golden coat felt softer than silk. Ella gazed around her, committing everything to memory so she could conjure up Blaze and the glade whenever she wanted.

He stamped an impatient foot and she laughed. "OK, let's go."

When Blaze turned towards the wildflower meadow Ella tugged his mane. She had a sudden urge to explore. "Let's go this way for a change," she said, guiding him towards the sea. He hesitated, his head high as he sniffed the faint traces of salt in the air.

"Come on," Ella urged, squeezing her legs and clicking her tongue. Blaze arched his neck and broke into a canter.

The scenery flashed by as the palomino pony lengthened his stride. Soon he was galloping flat out. The wind whipped past them, making Ella's eyes water, but she didn't care. She'd never ridden so fast in her life and the feeling of speed was exhilarating. Blaze galloped for miles, never seeming to tire, until the smell of the sea grew stronger and Ella could hear waves slapping against distant rocks.

Blaze slowed to a halt, his nostrils flaring. Ella slid to the ground and rested an arm on his neck. They were at the top of the cliffs close to The Lookout. She glanced over her shoulder and her eyes widened when she saw smoke curling from the chimney.

Below them the soporific sound of the sea made Ella's eyelids grow heavy.

"I mustn't fall asleep!" she cried, looking around her wildly. She spied a path that led down the side of the cliff. "Come on Blaze, let's explore."

The stony path was as wide as Ella's outstretched arms and hugged the sheer rock face like ivy on the broad bough of a tree. Blaze followed Ella as she picked her way down. Ella kept her eyes firmly ahead. If she peered over the edge at the swirling water below her stomach flipped alarmingly. At least the adrenalin that was coursing through her veins had banished any thoughts of sleep.

Every now and again she stopped, scratched Blaze's ears and whispered little words of encouragement.

After what seemed like hours the path flattened out and suddenly they were on a large slab of rock, pitted with pyramid-like limpets and clusters of mussels as black as grapes. On the far side of the rock was a perfect crescent of sand, pale yellow in the moonlight. It looked so inviting that Ella jumped down without thinking and sprinted from one end to the other. Blaze tossed his mane and cantered after her, his ears pricked and his tail high. Ella collapsed, laughing, in the sand, and Blaze stood beside her and stared out to sea.

"This is perfect," Ella told him softly. "I wish we could stay here forever."

Ella strolled along the beach examining shells and lengths of driftwood. Moonlight glittered on a small blue pebble by the water's edge. It was a piece of sea glass, worn smooth by the waves. Ella slipped it into the pocket of her pyjamas.

After a while she sat down, cross-legged, and

let fistfuls of sand run through her fingers as if her hands were an hourglass, measuring the time she had left with Blaze. Sensing her sadness, he nuzzled her cheek, blowing warm air into the nape of her neck until she giggled again.

Ella was so wrapped up in her pony that she didn't see the waves that lapped over the footprints they'd made in the sand just minutes before. Nor did she notice that the crescent of beach was becoming narrower as the tide raced in.

Blaze was the first to realise what had happened. His head shot up as he sniffed the wind and he whinnied. Ella looked around and cried out in shock.

The tide had come in, covering the slab of rock they'd climbed over to reach the beach. Behind them the vertical cliff face loomed over them, as high as a cathedral. In front of them the sea surged menacingly.

There was no way out. They were trapped.

15
Guardian Angel

Ella tried to think clearly. There must be a way. She squared her shoulders and stepped into the swirling sea. Just to see how deep it was, she told herself. Wet sand sucked at her feet like quicksand. Ella felt Blaze's eyes on her as she ploughed on until the water was churning around her knees.

She turned to look at the little palomino. As she did, a huge breaker rolled in and knocked her flying. Suddenly she was in the water, fighting for breath as the waves washed over her. Ella scrambled to her feet but another wave rolled in and sent her crashing to the ground again. Above the roaring of the sea

Ella heard a high-pitched whinny. Just like the bad dream, she thought in horror.

"It's OK. I'm OK," she spluttered. Her hair clung to her head like seaweed and her eyes stung with salty water. She crawled back onto the beach and slumped on the sand. Blaze whickered.

"Well, Plan A was a disaster," she said in a wobbly voice. "Maybe the water over the rock is shallow enough to paddle through."

But one glance told her all she needed to know - waves were crashing over the wide slab of rock they'd climbed over such a short time ago. If they tried to cross it now they would be swept straight out to sea.

She scoured the beach, desperately seeking a hidden cave, another set of steps, anything that could lead them to safety. She knew time was running out and soon the whole bay would be under water.

Ella remembered her dad's story about the time he and Aunt Rowan had been cut off by the tide. They'd climbed the cliff, hadn't they? She jumped to her feet and stared at the rock, looking for footholds. There were a few.

Enough to give her a fighting chance, anyway. And then she remembered Blaze, standing quietly behind her. There was no way she would ever leave him.

Swallowing the lump in her throat, Ella wrapped her arms around the palomino's neck.

"I don't know what to do," she muttered into his mane. "This dream has turned into a nightmare."

Blaze stepped away from her and walked over to the sea. "Don't leave me!" Ella cried, her voice carried away by the wind. She ran to his side. Water swirled around their feet as they sank in the sand. Ella cupped his face in her hands and gazed into his beautiful brown eyes. And then she remembered. Horses can swim. Suddenly she knew what they had to do.

Clambering onto Blaze's back, Ella took a deep breath and kicked him on. He plunged into the sea, sending beads of water flying through the air. Ella clung to his neck as he disappeared into the waves, just another white horse in the pounding surf. Battered and buffeted by the sea, Ella struggled to stay on his back. She realised he was swimming towards the bottom of the clifftop path.

"You can do it," she shouted above the roar of the waves. Blaze flicked an ear back and ploughed on, fighting to keep his head above water. Time stood still as he stretched for the shore. Ella could feel he was beginning to tire and squeezed her legs.

And then his hooves bit into the sand and he scrambled onto the path. Her heart bursting with pride, Ella slithered off and threw her arms around him.

"You did it, Blaze! You saved me."

The bed felt gritty. Ella grimaced and peered under the duvet. Grains of sand covered the sapphire blue sheet. She didn't even need to check her pocket to know that the piece of sea glass would be there. She sat on the end of her bed, reliving the dream. Blaze had saved her life. He was her guardian angel. And today she was going home without him. The thought of leaving him behind, locked inside his painting, broke her heart.

There was a gentle knock on the door and Aunt Rowan peered into the bedroom. "There you are!" she said. "I thought you'd gone to say goodbye to Alex."

Ella smiled weakly. "You finally remembered his name."

Aunt Rowan looked proud. "I did, didn't I? It's done me the power of good having you to stay." She frowned. "I'm really going to miss you."

Ella slid off the bed and gave her aunt a hug. "I'm going to miss you, too. And Tabitha and Alex." She glanced at the painting. "And the Midnight Pony," she added.

At the thought of leaving Blaze a single tear rolled down Ella's cheek. Aunt Rowan smiled down her long nose.

"Don't be sad, Ella dear. He'll be waiting for you here, where he belongs. Where you belong, too," she said quietly.

"What do you mean?" Ella asked, wiping her nose on her sleeve. "The Lookout's your home."

"But it will be yours one day. The house is passed down the female Morgan line, just like

81

the red hair and the painting."

Ella was stunned. If someone had told her a week ago that one day she'd inherit a ramshackle old house on the top of a cliff she'd have been horrified. But she'd grown to love the creaky floorboards, winding staircases, draughty windows and dark portraits of her stern-looking ancestors. The Lookout felt like, like...Ella thought hard and then realisation dawned on her. The Lookout felt like home.

"I don't know what to say," Ella told her aunt.

"Say you'll come and visit me and Blaze soon."

Ella felt as though she'd been hit by a steamroller.

"How do you know - ?"

"Blaze's name?" said her aunt. "Call it magic."

Ella glanced at the little palomino pony and shook her head sadly. "Sometimes I wish magic existed, Aunt Rowan, I really do. My best friend Molly believes in it. But, then again, she thinks you're a witch," said Ella unthinkingly.

Her aunt roared with laughter. "Does she now? And what do you think, Ella?"

Ella felt another tear slide down her cheek. "There's no such thing as magic."

Aunt Rowan lifted Ella's chin and looked her squarely in the eye. "Oh, but there is, my dear Ella. There is magic everywhere, if you just know where to look."

16

One Last Surprise

Ella stared blankly out of the window as the landscape raced past. In the front of the car her parents chatted about their trip. Usually Ella would be fascinated to hear tales about the Arctic foxes they'd been researching. But not today. Today all she could think about was Blaze.

How did Aunt Rowan know his name when Ella had called him that in a dream? Perhaps Alex had told her. But then Ella remembered that she'd never told Alex the name she'd given the Midnight Pony. Perhaps Ella had murmured it in her sleep when Aunt Rowan was in the room. Yes, that was the most likely explanation.

Ella's dad glanced at her in the rear view mirror. "Hey Ella, have I ever told you about the time - "

"You and Aunt Rowan got cut off by the tide and had to climb the cliff to safety?" Ella said tiredly. "More times than I can remember."

Her mum swivelled around in her seat. "Cheer up Ella, it might never happen."

"It already has," Ella muttered and stared blankly out of the window again. She must have dozed off, because when she woke up her dad was driving straight past the road that led to their house.

"Where are we going?"

"You'll see," said her dad, waving to Mrs Johnson as they passed the bakery.

Ella noticed her mum and dad exchange smiles. "What's going on?" she said, her eyebrows knotted in suspicion.

"Oh look, there's Molly," said her mum, ignoring her. Sure enough, Molly was tramping along the road in her jodhpurs, her riding hat tucked under her arm, obviously heading for Ivyleaf. Ella's mum wound her window down. "Hi Molly, do you want a lift?"

Molly beamed at them. "Yes please. I'm going to the stables if it's not out of your way?"

"It's not out of our way at all," said Ella's dad. "Hop in."

Molly slid into the seat next to Ella. "Missed you," she said.

"Missed you, too."

"Was it as bad as you thought it was going to be?"

The smell of the ocean filled Ella's nostrils as she remembered the puffins, the picnic on the beach, Aunt Rowan's strange meals and the midnight rides on Blaze. She smiled at her best friend, feeling her gloom lift a little. "Actually, it was alright."

"Here we are," said her dad, turning down the bumpy lane to the stables.

"Can I say a quick hello to Rocky?" asked Ella, already undoing her seatbelt.

"I don't see why not," said her mum. "We'll come, too."

Ella stared at her parents. Although they

both claimed to like horses it was usually from what they called a healthy distance.

Ella and Molly crossed the yard. Only Oscar, Mrs Bee's draft horse, looked over his stable door when he heard their footsteps.

"The ponies must be out," said Molly, reaching into the tack room for Henry's headcollar.

Behind her, Ella could hear her parents whispering furtively. When she turned to ask them what they were talking about their mouths clamped shut.

"Ah, there's Mrs Bee!" cried her dad. "You go and find the ponies. I need a quick word."

Ella pulled up a handful of grass and wondered if Rocky had missed her. She still had a couple of months left before he retired. She made up her mind to make the most of them.

Her dad joined them again. He gave Ella's mum a thumbs up.

"What's going on?" Ella said.

"You'll see," said her mum mysteriously.

"There they are," called Molly, pointing under the apple tree, still heavy with blossom.

Henry and Rocky were standing nose to tail, swishing flies, half asleep in the spring sunshine.

Ella remembered the first time she saw Blaze standing beneath the old oak tree in the glade and her eyes blurred with tears. The memory of the little palomino pony was so sharp it was as if she could actually see him, standing a little to the right of Henry's brown and white rump. Ella blinked away her tears and stared harder. There was a palomino pony standing with the other two. Her heart skipped a beat. Then she shook her head. She was probably just imagining things again.

And then Molly said, "Look, Mrs Bee must have bought a new pony to give lessons on. He's gorgeous."

Ella rubbed her eyes and gazed, open-mouthed, at the new pony. His coat was the colour of honey and his mane and tail were as white as newly-fallen snow.

Don't be stupid, said an unwelcome voice inside her head. It's a coincidence, that's all it is. Mrs Bee has just happened to buy a pony that looks a little bit like the one in your painting.

Ella quickened her pace, her eyes never leaving the little gelding. He had one white sock. Near fore.

Think logically - it can't be him, said the voice. Ignoring it Ella stepped up to the pony, uncurled her fingers and offered him the grass with a trembling hand. She hardly dared look, but when she did she gasped. Beneath his forelock was a blaze the shape of a bolt of lightning.

She gazed into his chocolate brown eyes and whispered, "Blaze, is it really you?"

Ella felt her dad's hand on her shoulder. "You can call him whatever you like, sweetheart. He's all yours."

Ella shook her head in disbelief. "I don't understand."

"He's your late birthday present," said her mum, giving the pony a tentative pat.

"We were going to get you a mountain bike," explained her dad. "I was literally about to order it when Rowan phoned and told me about this pony. He belonged to a friend of hers who was moving abroad and she needed to find him a new home fast. He was going for a song."

"But where will he live? We can't afford the livery fees!" cried Ella, not daring to build her hopes up.

"Rowan is paying them. She insisted."

Ella threw her arms around Blaze and he whickered softly. Time stood still as she clung to his neck, the others all but forgotten. He smelt of spring grass and wild flowers.

A terrible thought occurred to Ella. She pulled away, took a deep breath and pinched the soft skin on the inside of her thigh. "Ouch," she winced.

"What on earth are you doing?" said her mum.

"Just checking," said Ella, finally allowing herself to believe. Aunt Rowan was right. There was magic everywhere, if only you knew where to look.

"Checking what?" said Molly.

Ella kissed Blaze's soft nose tenderly and grinned at them all. "That I wasn't dreaming."

Juno's Foal

1

Summer on the Farm

Leah Lindberg was re-arranging her pony books in alphabetical order when her mum marched into her bedroom and ruined her summer.

"Dad and I are flying to the UK for a lecture tour on Monday. You're going to stay with your Aunt Freya while we're away. It's all arranged."

"What?" Leah spluttered, catching a glimpse of herself in her dressing table mirror. Her face had turned as white as her jodhpurs.

"I'm sorry to spring it on you darling, but it was too good an opportunity to turn down." Her mum didn't even have the grace to look abashed.

"I've never met Aunt Freya. She's not even my proper aunt!"

"She's your godmother, and you have met her, although you were probably too young to remember. That's why I thought it would be a lovely opportunity to get to know her and the twins."

"The twins?" Leah sat down on her bed with a thump. She'd forgotten about Oscar and Isabella.

"They must be eight now. Only a year younger than you. You'll have a fantastic summer, I promise you."

Leah was about to protest. But her mum had already turned on her heels and disappeared out of the room.

Leah picked her way through the puddles on the rutted track to the riding school and tried to ignore the feeling of gloom that clung to her like a limpet. She'd been looking forward to the summer holidays for weeks, especially after her mum had agreed she could help out at the stables every weekend. Instead she was being sent to her godmother's farm miles away. It wasn't fair.

Her heart gave a little leap when she saw Sparkle tied up outside his stable, his grey head buried in a haynet. She reached in the pocket of her jodhpurs for a carrot and whistled. Sparkle turned his head, saw her and whinnied. Leah flung her arms around his neck and tried not to think about how much she'd miss him.

She jumped when a girl's face appeared over Sparkle's withers. The girl had streaks of mud on her cheeks and so much hay sticking out of her tousled brown hair that she could have passed for a human haynet. Her navy jodhpurs and shirt were covered in dust.

"Hello!" said the girl. "I'm Lisa. Are you Leah?"

Leah nodded and squirmed as Lisa looked her up and down.

"Sam said you have a lesson at ten. Sparkle's all ready for you."

"Thanks. He looks great." Leah offered Sparkle the carrot and he picked it daintily from her palm. She smiled as his whiskers tickled her fingers, not noticing that Lisa was still staring at her, her eyes wide.

"How on earth do you manage to keep so clean?" Lisa asked.

Leah looked down. Her jodhpurs were freshly-laundered and as white as Sparkle's immaculately-groomed flanks. Her black leather boots were so shiny she could see her face in them. She shrugged. "Not sure. I just do."

"Lucky you. My mum's always giving me grief for being so scruffy. Yesterday she threatened to hose me down before she let me in the house," Lisa laughed. "Sam said you're helping out this summer, too."

Leah's face clouded over. "Not any more. I'm going to stay with my godmother on her farm. I've only just found out."

"That's a shame. Still, summer on a farm sounds like fun. Does she have horses?"

Leah thought hard. She knew Freya had cattle and sheep. She seemed to remember there were chickens, too. But no-one had ever mentioned horses.

"I don't think so," she said glumly. Sparkle

nuzzled her pockets. On the other side of the yard Sam, the riding school's owner, was opening the gate into the menage.

"You'd better go or you'll be in trouble. You know how much Sam hates people being late for lessons," Lisa said, reaching for a yard broom.

Leah flashed her a grateful smile. She adjusted the stirrups, checked Sparkle's girth and swung into the saddle. She gathered her reins and was turning the little grey pony towards the menage when a thought struck her.

"Lisa?"

Lisa stopped sweeping. "What's up?"

"Will you look after Sparkle while I'm away? Make sure he gets lots of attention? I'm going to miss him so much." Leah's eyes prickled with unshed tears. She reached for the handkerchief in her pocket and blew her nose.

"Of course I will. I'll give him a cuddle three times a day and tell him it's from you."

"And a carrot," Leah said with a watery smile. "He loves carrots."

Lisa nodded, stroking Sparkle's soft nose.

"Carrots and cuddles. No problem."

Leah's gloom lifted a fraction. At least she was leaving Sparkle in good hands.

2
Hollow End

Freya and her twins Isabella and Oscar lived on a remote farm a four hour drive from the city where Leah had lived all her life. Freya and Leah's mum had been friends since university but although they talked regularly on the phone they hadn't seen each other for years.

Leah's stomach churned at the thought of spending the entire summer with people she didn't know. What if her godmother was strict and the twins were horrible? There was a photo above the fireplace of Freya holding Leah at her christening. Leah was wearing a white christening gown and a beaming smile, her chubby fists waving at the camera as Freya gazed at her fondly. Her godmother had shoulder-length dark brown hair, wide-set grey eyes and a crinkly smile. Leah had to admit that she didn't look strict, but you never knew.

Her mum caught her studying the photo that evening.

"Don't worry Leah, you'll love Freya," she said. "And if the twins are anything like their mum, you'll love them too."

"Where's their dad?"

"He and Freya divorced about five years ago. That's when she moved to the farm."

"Does she have any horses?"

Her mum sighed. "Life doesn't revolve around horses, Leah."

Leah stuck out her chin. "It does for me."

Two days later Leah was sitting in the back of the car, her suitcase beside her, trying to calm her nerves as the countryside sped past.

"Not long now," said her dad, watching her in the rear-view mirror.

"What time's your plane?" Leah asked.

"Not 'til seven," said her mum.

"Make sure you get seats by the emergency exit," Leah reminded them.

Leah wasn't a pessimist. She just liked to be prepared. She listened to safety talks on planes and ferries and always checked where fire exits were when she visited somewhere new. She knew how to put someone in the recovery position and could list where every single fire extinguisher was kept in her school. Her parents thought it wasn't normal behaviour for a nine-year-old but Leah didn't care. If she was going to be stuck on a plane with engine trouble she wanted to know exactly how to inflate her life-jacket.

"There's the turning," said her dad, pointing to a roughshod lane which looped away to their left. Leah craned her neck to catch a glimpse of the farm. They passed a handpainted sign propped against a weathered five bar gate. Hollow End. Leah shivered in spite of the warmth of the car. It sounded like the end of the world.

The car slowed to a halt outside a rambling wooden farmhouse that had been painted sage green. Leah flicked a speck of fluff from her favourite red shorts and smoothed her hair self-consciously. Before she could undo her seatbelt two rosy-faced children appeared outside her window. One opened the passenger door and the other beckoned her out.

"I'm Oscar," said the boy. "And that's -"

"Isabella," finished the girl. "We've been waiting for you for ages."

Her godmother stepped forward, her tanned face creased in a smile. "And you probably don't remember me, but I'm Freya."

Leah held out her hand politely but Freya ignored her and swept her into a hug. She smelt of newly-cut hay and molasses and her faded checked cotton shirt had been washed so many times it was soft against Leah's cheek.

"Look at you, all grown up! It's been too long."

The twins disappeared into a barn behind them and Leah stood awkwardly while Freya and her parents chatted about the journey. She almost jumped out of her skin when she felt something warm and furry rub against her knee. She looked down to see a ginger farm cat weaving between her legs, purring loudly.

"That's Marmalade," said Oscar, reappearing with his sister, who was carrying a clear plastic box filled with mud. Leah bent down to tickle Marmalade's chin.

"We've made something for you," Isabella said, thrusting the box into Leah's hands. "It's a worm farm! We've been collecting them all day."

Leah took the box hesitantly and held it at arm's length, trying not to look at the pink-skinned earthworms writhing and tunnelling in the crumbly soil.

"Thank you," she said. "I think."

Her dad checked his watch. "We'd better be off otherwise we'll miss the flight." He unloaded Leah's bags from the car and carried them to the back door.

"Be good for Freya," said her mum, kissing her cheek. "We'll see you in six weeks."

"Good luck with the lecture tour," Leah mumbled. She watched her parents' car wind its way along the twisting farm track and out of sight. A wave of homesickness washed over her. Freya patted her shoulder and smiled.

"We're so happy that you're spending the summer with us, aren't we kids?"

The twins nodded.

"We'll show you your room," said Isabella. "We've made a space for the worm farm on your bedside table. We thought you'd like them nice and close."

Leah cast one last look at the track and followed Freya and the twins into the farmhouse with heavy steps.

3

Juno's Secret

Leah's room was at the back of the house, looking out onto a field of sheep. It was a small, square room with plain whitewashed walls, simple wooden furniture and red and white checked curtains. Freya had left a small vase of wild flowers on the chest of drawers. Oscar placed the worm farm on the bedside table and gazed at it lovingly.

"You need to keep the soil moist otherwise they'll dry out," he said, wiggling his fingers in the mud.

Leah shuddered. How on earth was she ever going to sleep with a boxful of worms a few centimetres from her head? Freya must have noticed her unease because she picked the box up and handed it back to her son.

"For heaven's sake Oscar, Leah doesn't want worms in her room. Keep them on the window ledge on the landing if you must." Freya fixed her son with a steely gaze and he scooted out of the room, the worm farm cradled in his arms.

Leah unzipped her suitcase. Freya waved her hand. "Leave the unpacking until later. We'll give you a guided tour of the farm and introduce you to Juno."

"Who's Juno?" Leah asked, as they crossed the farmyard past a handful of chickens enjoying a dust bath in the sunshine.

"You'll see," said Isabella, tapping her nose. "But you're going to love her."

Three goats were nibbling the grass in a small paddock to one side of the house. "Is she a goat?" Leah asked.

Isabella giggled. "No."

They passed a pig ark surrounded by a sea of mud. Snouting around in the dirt were a dozen tiny piglets who squealed with excitement when they saw Freya and the twins.

"It's not tea time yet," Oscar told them.

"Is Juno a pig?" Leah asked. Oscar shook his head and chuckled.

They walked through a field of golden wheat and another where the grass was so long it reached Leah's knees.

"We'll be cutting this for hay in the next week or so," said Freya. She pointed out the sheep and cows and showed Leah the tractor barn and the caravans where the two farmhands, Eric and Joseph, lived. Leah's new trainers were coated in grime by the time they had toured the whole farm. They were almost right back where they'd started and there was still no sign of the mysterious Juno.

Then Leah noticed a small weather-boarded building to the side of the barn. A leather headcollar was hanging on a hook beside the stable door. She crossed her fingers.

"Follow me," Isabella said, tugging Leah's hand.

They stood on tiptoes and peered into the stable. Standing in a deep bed of straw was a chestnut pony with a flaxen mane and tail.

Leah clicked her tongue and the pony turned and whickered softly.

"That's Juno," said Oscar.

Juno wandered over and let Leah stroke her soft nose.

"Mum's had her since she was a foal," said Isabella proudly.

"She's beautiful," said Leah. "Horses are my favourite animals."

"I know, your mum told me," said Freya. "We all have jobs on the farm. Isabella feeds the chickens and collects the eggs. Oscar is in charge of the goats and Eric, Joseph and I look after the cattle, sheep and pigs. I thought you might like to take care of Juno while you're here."

Leah gazed at the chestnut pony. "I would love to," she breathed.

"She's got bad feet so she can't be ridden but she loves being groomed and made a fuss of, and she'll happily go for a walk on the lead rein," her godmother said.

The twins tied Juno up outside her stable and Freya eyed her critically.

"She could certainly do with the exercise.

She's been on a strict diet for weeks and just keeps getting fatter and fatter. I can't understand it. If I didn't know better, I'd say you two horrors had been feeding her titbits on the sly."

Leah was surprised to see the twins shoot each other guilty looks. She turned back to Juno, whose stomach was as tight and round as a barrel. Sam had a couple of brood mares at the riding stables that produced long-legged fillies and colts every summer. Leah recognised the signs.

Juno wasn't fat. She was in foal.

4

Neat-Freak

Isabella sat on the end of Leah's bed and watched in fascination as she unpacked her suitcase. On the landing they could hear Oscar murmuring to the worms.

"Did your mum pack your case?" Isabella asked.

"No, I did. Why d'you ask?" Leah said, refolding a tee-shirt and placing it carefully in a drawer.

"It's just so neat."

"I like it like that."

Isabella picked up a small framed photo of Sparkle peering over his stable door. "Who's that?"

"The pony I ride at the stables. I was going to be helping there this summer."

"He's pretty." Isabella studied the photo, tracing Sparkle's face with her finger. "You don't want to be here, do you?" she said matter-of-factly.

Leah felt a dark flush creep up her neck. "I do," she lied.

Isabella handed Leah the photo. "I was really excited when Mum said you were coming. I thought we could be friends. Oscar's alright, but he is a boy. And you know how annoying boys can be."

"I heard that," said a voice from the landing.

"But you don't like it here, I can tell."

"I'm just a bit homesick," said Leah. "I'll be fine." She bent her head over her suitcase, wondering how she could change the subject. A whinny rang out across the farmyard. Leah took a deep breath and blurted, "Why haven't you told your mum that Juno's in foal?"

It was Isabella's turn to look uncomfortable.

"I don't know what you're talking about. She's just a bit tubby, that's all."

Leah lay on her bed, staring at the ceiling and trying not to think about home. After denying that Juno was in foal Isabella had muttered something about collecting the eggs and disappeared, closing the door behind her. Leah had heard her whispering to Oscar on the landing. She'd tiptoed over and pressed her ear against the knotted pine door.

"What if she tells Mum?" Oscar's voice was anxious.

"Shh! Keep your voice down. We just deny it, remember."

"Mum's going to find out sooner or later. Perhaps we should tell her first?"

"No way," Isabella said firmly. "Follow me. I've got an idea how we can make Miss Neat Freak feel more at home on the farm."

Leah clasped the photo of Sparkle to her chest and a single tear rolled down her cheek. She longed to throw her arms around the little grey gelding's neck and bury her face in his silver mane. The urge to be with a pony - any pony - was overwhelming.

She stood up and brushed away the tear. She would visit Juno. Juno would make everything alright.

But when Leah stuck her head over Juno's stable door five minutes later the mare was nowhere to be seen.

"She's in the orchard," said Freya, appearing from the hay barn.

"I wondered if she'd like a groom," Leah said.

"I'm sure she would. Come with me."

Leah followed Freya into a small lean-to at the back of the barn. Feed bins lined one side and the other was piled high with spare buckets and feeding troughs. The sweet smell of freshly-baled hay filled Leah's nostrils. Freya handed her a bucket filled with brushes and Juno's leather headcollar.

They crossed the yard, climbed over a five bar gate and followed a rutted track to an old apple orchard. Juno stood dozing in the shade of one of the trees.

Leah hesitated. Sparkle was always tacked up when she arrived for her weekly riding lesson. She'd never actually groomed a pony before, let alone caught one and put on its headcollar.

Sensing her worries her godmother smiled. "Would you like me to show you what to do?"

Leah nodded.

"Juno's very easy to catch. She'll do anything for a carrot," Freya said, producing one from the pocket of her jeans and giving it to Leah. They tramped across the grass to the mare, who opened one eye and whickered sleepily. Leah held out her hand and gave Juno the carrot while Freya looped the lead rope over the mare's neck to stop her walking away. She showed Leah how to slip the noseband over Juno's muzzle and pass the headpiece over her poll. Leah buckled the strap and Juno gave her a friendly nudge. They led her over to the fence.

"I know how to do a quick release knot. I watched a video on YouTube and practised with the cord of my dressing gown," said Leah.

Freya reached into her pocket and pulled out a length of baler twine which she circled around one of the wooden fence rails and tied fast with a knot. "You should never tie a horse directly to a gate or fence because if they panic and pull back they could hurt themselves. Tie her up to the baler twine instead. That way, if she pulls back the string will break."

Leah pictured her pink dressing gown cord. Her brow furrowed in concentration as she tied a quick release knot.

"Good job," said Freya. She glanced at her watch. "I'd better be getting on. That's if you're OK here?"

Leah ran her hand down Juno's chestnut neck. She felt happy for the first time since she'd arrived at Hollow End Farm.

"Yes," she grinned. "I'll be OK."

5

Meeting Matilda

Leah tipped the bucket of brushes onto the grass and took stock. Two dandy brushes, one body brush, a mane comb, a rubber curry comb, a metal curry comb and a hoof pick. They were all filthy. She set to work, using the metal curry comb to clean the dirt, dust and hairs from the brushes, whistling as she did.

"Isabella thinks I'm a neat freak, just because I like things clean and tidy," she said to Juno, who cocked a chestnut ear back to listen. "I can't help it. It's just the way I am."

Once the brushes were clean Leah picked up the body brush and began brushing Juno's neck, using the same circular strokes she'd seen the stablehands using when they were grooming the riding school ponies. She tried not to notice the layer of dust that settled on her like a veil. But she couldn't ignore the taste of grit in her mouth and pulled a face as she ran her tongue around her lips.

"The cleaner you are, the dirtier I'm getting," she told Juno, grimacing as she ran her hand down the mare's near foreleg towards her muddy hoof. Juno obliged by lifting it for her. Leah cupped the hoof in her left hand and, holding the hoofpick in her right hand, carefully picked the mud from around the frog, just as the stablehands did. Juno nibbled at her lead rope as Leah picked out her other three feet.

She was just wiping her hands on a tussock of grass when Oscar appeared.

"Mum says can you feed the piglets?" he said.

"Sure. I'm just about finished here." Leah stood back and admired her handiwork. Juno's chestnut coat gleamed. She undid Juno's headcollar and the mare ambled over to the mud by the water trough. Leah watched with resignation as Juno grunted, sank to her knees and rolled, wriggling on her back, her legs waving in the air, as she rubbed mud into her mane with abandon. She stood and shook from head to hoof, sending a cloud of dust flying through the air.

"That was a waste of time," Oscar remarked.

Leah sighed and was about to agree when she realised how much she'd enjoyed grooming Juno. And how much the mare had enjoyed the attention.

"Actually it wasn't." She gathered the brushes and climbed over the gate to join Oscar. "You'd better show me what needs doing."

The piglets were rootling around in the mud when Leah arrived with the bucket of pellets Oscar had given her. Their trough was on the far side of their pen and Leah climbed the fence, the bucket swinging at her side. As soon as they saw her the piglets barrelled over, falling over each other in their hurry to reach her.

"Here you go," Leah said, pouring the pellets

into the trough. She watched them snuffle up their supper. The piglets were small enough to cup in two hands. "You really are too cute," she told them.

As she turned to go Leah became aware of heavy breathing coming from the pig ark behind her. Puzzled, she looked over her shoulder. She gasped. Barging her way out of the ark was a sow the size of a small Shetland pony and she was heading straight for Leah, her eyes fixed on the empty bucket in Leah's hands. The sow gave an angry squeal and Leah's legs turned to jelly. As she started running for the fence she chanced another look back. It was a mistake. She tripped over one of the piglets and fell flat on her face in the mud. Covering her ears to drown out the noise of the sow's thundering feet, Leah opened her lungs and screamed.

Leah felt a tapping on her shoulder. And then someone gently prised her fingers away from her ears.

"It's OK, you're fine," said her godmother. "Here, take my hand."

Leah did as she was told and Freya pulled her to her feet. The sow was snouting around by her side. Leah shrank back and her mud-splattered face paled.

"Don't worry, Matilda's harmless. She was after the bucket, not you," Freya said. "Let's get you back to the house. I think you could probably do with a shower and a change of clothes."

Oscar and Isabella were hanging on the gate, watching.

"Did Oscar forget to tell you about Matilda?" Isabella asked innocently.

Leah brushed mud from her eyelashes and met the other girl's eyes. She knew Isabella was testing her, to see if she would tell tales.

"No, it was my fault. She just caught me by surprise."

Isabella nodded approvingly and jumped off the gate. "Want to help me clean out the hen house? It's a really smelly job."

Leah glanced down. She was covered in mud from head to toe. A bit of chicken manure wasn't going to make much difference. She had a sudden urge to giggle.

"Why not? As long as I can have a peg for my nose."

Mucking out the chickens was a turning point for Leah and Isabella and by the time they came in for dinner a couple of hours later they were firm friends.

"I'm sorry we sent you in with Matilda," Isabella said, as they headed for bed that night. "We knew she wouldn't hurt you."

"That's OK," said Leah. "And I'm sorry, too. You were right. I didn't want to come here. But now I think I might enjoy the summer after all."

6

A Walk to the River

Leah soon fell into the rhythms of Hollow End Farm. In the mornings she and the twins helped Freya feed the cows and sheep and picked vegetables from the farm's kitchen garden. They spent the long warm afternoons with Juno, grooming her, taking her for walks on the farm or just lying in the grass with the sun on their faces while the mare grazed quietly beside them.

Leah didn't mention Juno's expanding stomach again. She didn't want to spoil things. Anyway, what if she was wrong? She didn't want to wreck her friendship with Isabella and Oscar. Perhaps the lush grass was making the mare fat.

One afternoon towards the end of Leah's second week at Hollow End the three children were in the apple orchard. Isabella and Oscar were dangling from a rope swing they'd hung from a branch while Leah combed the tangles from Juno's long flaxen mane.

She was running a hand over the mare's belly when something jabbed her palm. She called out in surprise.

"What's up," said Oscar, who was hanging upside down from the rope.

"I felt something move in Juno's tummy," Leah said.

"Probably wind," said Isabella.

"It was more like a kick. Come and feel."

Isabella reluctantly untangled herself from the swing and placed a hand on Juno's stomach. "Can't feel anything. You must have imagined it," she said.

"I didn't. It definitely moved. Look! It's doing it again."

Together they watched the mare's flanks ripple. Isabella glanced at her brother.

"Just tell her," he said.

Isabella took a deep breath. "You were right. We do think she might be having a baby."

"Don't you think you should tell your mum?"

"She'll have a meltdown. She's got enough to do with the calves and lambs without worrying about a foal," said Oscar.

"But she's going to find out soon anyway," Leah pointed out.

"We thought we'd wait until the foal was born and then tell her." Isabella stroked Juno's flank. "It'll be too late for her to do anything about it by then."

It was only that night as she drifted off to sleep that Leah realised she'd forgotten to ask the twins one important question. Who was the father of Juno's foal?

There was no sign of Isabella and Oscar at breakfast the following morning.

"They had an early start," said Freya. "It's their weekend at their dad's. They'll be back on Sunday evening."

After she'd helped feed the animals Leah

decided to take Juno for a walk.

"Where does the bottom gate in the orchard go?" she asked her godmother.

"If you follow the track to the lane and turn right it'll take you to the river. It's a nice walk, but don't go near the mudflats, whatever you do. They're like quicksand. It's so easy to sink down into the mud and get stuck."

Leah was slowly becoming used to the mud on the farm, but she was happy to give the mudflats a wide berth. "Don't worry, I won't."

Juno whickered when Leah appeared with a headcollar in one hand and a carrot in the other, and gave a contented sigh as Leah scratched her poll.

"We're going for a walk," Leah told her, slipping the headcollar on. She clicked her tongue and Juno followed her through the bottom gate and onto a narrow stony track.

Progress was slow because Juno stopped every few yards to nibble the frothy white cow parsley growing in the hedgerows. Leah didn't mind - the afternoon stretched ahead of her, empty and inviting. They reached the lane. Just as they were about to turn right a poster on a telegraph pole directly ahead of them caught Leah's eye. She tugged the lead rope and Juno waddled after her, her round belly swinging with each step.

The poster was bleached by the sun and its tattered edges flapped in the wind. Narrowing her eyes, Leah read the faded print.

"Endo's Circus," she whispered, her index finger tracing the words. "It was here last August, look." Juno pricked her ears and listened to Leah as she read from the poster. "'Death defying acrobatics, daredevil jugglers and the most daring and dangerous equestrian act you will ever see. Watch in awe as Lightning the Wonder Horse leaps through a ring of fire.' It sounds amazing," Leah said. "There's a picture of him, too. He's beautiful."

Leah studied the poster. A Cremello stallion, his glossy coat the colour of vanilla ice cream, was standing on his hind-legs, his forelegs pawing the air. Behind him Leah could just about make out orange flames flickering around a giant hoop. "Imagine jumping through that. He must be so brave."

Juno stamped her hoof impatiently. Leah

smiled. "Sorry Juno. I promised you a walk, didn't I? Come on, let's go."

Soon the gunmetal grey river came into view, sandwiched between the wide mudflats Freya had warned were so dangerous. Leah found a ribbon of grass and sat cross-legged staring at the river as it meandered by, daydreaming about beautiful Cremello stallions while Juno grazed peacefully by her side.

7
Echo

Leah woke with a start, her heart thudding. Someone had turned on her bedside light and was shaking her shoulder.

"Is it a fire?" Leah cried, throwing off her bedclothes and reaching for her jeans.

"No!" hissed Isabella, her finger on her lips. "Keep your voice down or you'll wake Mum."

"Then why on earth have you woken me at - " Leah squinted at the clock next to her bed, "one o'clock in the morning?"

"It's Juno," Isabella whispered urgently. "We think she's about to have the foal. Oscar's with her."

"Juno?" Leah pulled a sweatshirt over her

head and began lacing her trainers. "Why didn't you say? Let's go."

They crept out of the house and stole across the moonlit farmyard to Juno's stable. Oscar was leaning against the stable door, his face anxious. Inside Juno paced restlessly to and fro. Her chestnut flanks were dark with sweat. She saw Leah and Isabella and gave a shrill whinny.

"It's OK girl, you'll be alright," Leah murmured. The mare's brown eyes were full of trust.

"Do you think we should go in with her?" Oscar asked.

"No. She knows what to do, don't you Juno?" Leah said.

Juno grunted softly and lay down in her thick bed of straw. The moon disappeared behind a cloud and the stable fell into darkness. Leah felt Isabella's hand in hers and gave it a reassuring squeeze.

The three children stood quietly as the minutes ticked by, listening to the rustle of straw and Juno's laboured breathing. Just when Leah thought she couldn't wait a second longer the moon came out, casting a silver glow into Juno's stable. There, lying next to his mother, was a tiny palomino foal. The children gasped in delight.

"He's beautiful!" marvelled Leah.

Hearing her voice, the colt foal staggered to his feet. His spindly legs looked far too fragile to bear his weight. He stood unsteadily for a few seconds, wobbled alarmingly and crumpled back into the straw. Juno turned her head and gave him the gentlest of nudges. He gathered his strength and lurched to his feet again. Leah realised she was holding her breath.

"Come on boy, you can do it," she murmured. He swayed, tottered for a few shaky steps and collapsed again.

Juno heaved herself to her feet and the gangly colt foal followed suit. This time he managed half a dozen steps before sinking to the floor.

"He's getting stronger every time," said Oscar, a look of wonder on his face.

"What shall we call him?" Isabella asked.

"How about Frank?" said Oscar.

Isabella shook her head and Leah snorted with laughter. "That's a terrible name."

"Alright then, you think of one," Oscar said grumpily.

Leah gazed at the tiny foal and thought hard. "What about Echo?"

"I like it," said Isabella. "What do you think, Oscar?"

"It's alright, I suppose."

"It suits him," said Isabella.

"It's funny, but he reminds me of the horse on the poster for Endo's Circus," said Leah. "You know the one I mean? The Cremello stallion who jumps through hoops of fire."

"Echo's coat is darker," Isabella said, not meeting Leah's eyes.

"Not much." Leah pictured the faded poster, wondering why the twins were looking so shifty. And suddenly everything fell into place. "The circus came last August," she said, counting on her fingers. "That's eleven months ago."

"So?" muttered Oscar.

"Lightning is Echo's dad, isn't he?"

Oscar cast a sidelong look at his twin. Isabella shrugged. "We're not one hundred per cent sure. But we think he probably is."

"How on earth -?" began Leah.

"It was the night we went to the circus. We'd been looking forward to it for ages," said Oscar. "We were in such a hurry we couldn't have shut the gate to the orchard properly. When we took Juno her breakfast the next morning the gate was wide open and she'd vanished."

"What did your mum say?"

"She hadn't noticed," said Isabella. "We were going to tell her, really we were, but she'd been up all night calving and was having a lie-in."

"Then, while we were searching the farm for Juno -"

"Hugo turned up with her," said Isabella.

"Who on earth is Hugo?" asked Leah.

"The boy from the circus. The one who does all the riding tricks. He said he'd found her in Lightning's paddock." Isabella rested her chin on the stable door, watching Echo settle in the straw and fall asleep.

"We decided not to mention it to Mum because we thought it would all be OK. And then Juno started getting fatter and fatter and fatter -" said Oscar.

"And now she's had Echo we've got some serious explaining to do," finished his sister morosely.

8

A Model Pupil

Freya stood, open-mouthed, at the stable door. "Tell me I'm dreaming."

"I know. It was a shock for us, too," said Oscar.

"But I don't understand how -"

"It's a complete mystery," agreed Isabella. "But now he's here I suppose there's not much we can do about it. By the way, we've called him Echo."

"Echo," said Freya faintly. She looked completely flummoxed.

Earlier, as dawn's pink fingers had crept across the horizon, Isabella had made Leah promise not to tell Freya about Juno escaping to the circus.

"I hate lying," Leah had told her.

"It's not a lie. It's more a case of not mentioning the truth," Isabella had replied.

"But don't you think she'll guess as soon as she sees him? He looks so like his dad," Leah had argued weakly.

"Mum was too busy with the calving to go to the circus last year. Grandma and Grandpa took us. She never saw Lightning."

And now Freya was lost for words.

"We'll look after him," said Isabella. "You won't have to do a thing."

Echo tottered to the stable door and sniffed cautiously at Freya's hand. It was as if he knew he had to win her affections. Leah held her breath.

"He is very sweet," her godmother sighed. "Alright, I suppose he can stay."

The three children danced around the farmyard in delight, scattering chickens and sending Marmalade scurrying for cover. Juno watched them from over the stable door, wondering what all the fuss was about.

The next day Freya and the children drove to the animal feed store and bought a soft leather halter and a book on caring for foals.

"It says here that foals can gallop when they are a day old," said Isabella on the journey home. "That's amazing."

"That's because they need to be able to escape from predators like lions and wolves," said her brother.

"It's a good job there aren't any predators at Hollow End Farm - you two didn't take your first steps until you were a year old," said Freya, pulling onto the farm track.

"Horses are way cooler than humans, Mum," Oscar told her. "Did you know foals are born with all their senses, not like puppies or kittens which are born deaf and blind?"

"And a newborn foal's legs are almost as long as a fully-grown horse's legs," read Leah over Isabella's shoulder. "No wonder Echo has trouble folding his legs when he lies down."

Freya turned off the engine and swivelled in her seat so she could see Leah and the twins.

"It's a long time since Juno was Echo's age,

but I do remember how important it is to handle a foal as much as possible, and not to teach them any bad habits. We want Echo to grow into a happy and well-behaved horse, don't we?"

The three children nodded earnestly.

"Summer's a busy time of year on the farm and I'm not going to be able to spend much time with him, so I'm going to have to find someone else to start his training for me."

The twins looked crestfallen. Only Leah noticed her godmother's mouth twitch.

"Can you think of anyone who might want the job?" Freya asked.

"We'll do it!" Isabella blurted.

"We'll read the book from cover to cover and do everything it says," cried Oscar.

Freya nodded. "And you Leah, would you like to help?"

"More than anything," she said simply.

"Looks like I've found myself three horse trainers," said Freya with a satisfied smile. "I didn't think I'd have to look too far."

And so Echo's training began. Every day

Leah, Isabella and Oscar took it in turns to put the halter on the foal and lead him around the orchard. At first he skittered and jumped and barged into them, stepping on their toes and pulling against the lead rope.

"He's out of control. He's a hooligan foal," complained Isabella one evening, rubbing her bruised shin. Echo had spooked at a pheasant that afternoon, pulling so hard on his lead rope that Isabella had fallen headlong into the grass. The lead rope had slithered out of her hands and Echo had charged around the orchard for an hour before they'd managed to catch him again.

"You need to be patient. He's only a baby," said Freya.

The children persevered, rewarding Echo with praise and pats when he behaved himself and telling him off when he nipped and pushed. They stroked him from his ears to his tail, brushed him gently and ran their hands down his legs and picked up his feet so he was used to being handled. His attention span was short, so they kept their training sessions short, too.

When they led Juno out of the stable every morning Echo would trot obediently by the mare's side until they reached the orchard. Then he would stop, sniff the air and gallop through the apple trees, his nostrils flared. He would twist his body in a series of crazy leaps and bucks that made the children giggle. And then he would re-join Juno, picking at the grass by her feet as if he'd been by her side all along.

Slowly Echo learnt to walk calmly when he was being led, and how to stand on three legs when someone picked up one of his feet. He learnt that barging wasn't polite, but that if he was well-behaved he would be rewarded with a welcome scratch on his withers. He followed the children around the farmyard, snorting, goggle-eyed, at the piglets and cavorting with the lambs. Marmalade would jump from his favourite spot under the kitchen windowsill and weave around Echo's legs, purring loudly, whenever the foal appeared.

Echo was cheeky and fearless, affectionate and funny. Everyone fell head over heels in love with him.

9

A Night at the Circus

"**I** have some exciting news," announced
Freya one morning. "The circus is coming this
weekend!"

"Endo's Circus?" said Leah, an image of
Lightning popping into her head.

"That's right. I've booked us tickets for
Saturday's show."

"Are you sure you can spare the time?" said
Isabella, her face pale. "Grandma and
Grandpa could always take us if it's easier."

"Anyone would think you didn't want me to
come," said Freya, looking disappointed. "I
missed it last year. I don't want to miss it
again. It'll be a lovely family outing."

"Mum's going to take one look at Lightning and put two and two together," said Oscar, as he watched Leah and Isabella lead Echo around the orchard that afternoon.

Oscar was right, thought Leah. Every day the little palomino colt looked more like his father. Perhaps it was in the regal way he arched his neck. Maybe it was the way he carried his tail so proudly. But there was no doubting his princely bloodlines.

"It's a shame Echo will never get to meet his father," Leah said.

Isabella stopped so suddenly the little foal bumped into her. Her eyes took on a faraway look as she stroked his neck absentmindedly.

"Perhaps one day he will."

Leah had a sneaking suspicion that the twins were up to something, although she had no idea what it could be. But she kept finding them huddled together in corners, whispering urgently to each other. When she tackled Oscar about it while they mucked out Juno's stable he'd looked over his shoulder furtively and had beckoned her closer, as if he was about to confide in her. Then Isabella appeared with a bucket of water, shot him a warning look and the moment was gone.

On Friday evening Leah felt a flutter of excitement as she saw six brightly-coloured lorries lumber past the farm on their way to the field where the circus was being held. She shouted to the twins and they ran over and watched for an hour as people dressed in tee-shirts and shorts jumped from the cabs of their lorries and started erecting the huge blue and red big top.

"It's funny to think that on Saturday night they'll be acrobats, jugglers and clowns in fancy costumes," said Leah. "They look very ordinary today."

There was no sign of Lightning or Hugo.

"What if they're not coming this year?" Oscar fretted.

His sister climbed the gate into the field and marched over to a portly man with a thatch of silver hair. She pointed at the big tent and he shook his head.

"What did he say?" Oscar asked as Isabella

tramped back.

"Lightning was a bit lame this morning. Hugo's had to take him to the vets. They're not sure if he'll make tomorrow's show."

Freya looked at the clock above the woodburner.

"It's a quarter to six. Time to go."

The twins were unusually quiet as they walked along the lane to the big top and joined the queue of people lining up outside. A girl in a sparkly pink leotard checked their tickets.

"You're in the front row, seats twenty to twenty three," she told them.

"Where's the emergency exit?" Leah asked.

The girl looked perplexed. "It's a tent. There isn't one."

"Everything alright, Leah?" Freya looked at her in concern.

Leah reddened. "Yes, it's fine. I usually check when I go somewhere new, that's all. Mum says I worry too much but I say it's better to be safe than sorry."

"No need to worry tonight. Nothing can go

wrong with a trip to the circus," Freya assured her.

The girl in the sparkly leotard nodded. "And we always keep a couple of buckets of sand and a fire extinguisher by the entrance just in case."

"Is Lightning in the show tonight?" Isabella asked.

The girl smiled and nodded. "He certainly is. He's the last act to perform."

The children followed Freya into the tent and found their seats. "Who's sitting where?" she asked them.

Leah noticed Isabella elbow her brother in the ribs.

"I want to sit by the aisle," Oscar said.

Leah settled in the seat next to her godmother and gazed around her. The red and white striped roof of the big top was strung with fairy lights. A tightrope and a trapeze hung high above her head. The air fizzed with excitement as everyone waited for the show to start.

The ringmaster strode in and cracked a long black whip to deafening applause. He looked familiar, although Leah couldn't place him. And then she realised it was the man with the thatch of silver hair Isabella had spoken to the evening before. She hadn't recognised him in his top hat and crimson jacket.

"Ladies and gentleman, welcome to Endo's Circus, the greatest show on earth!" he cried. Suddenly the ring was filled with acrobats, jugglers, stilt-walkers and clowns. Leah watched, mesmerised, as a girl swung upside down from the trapeze and a man on a unicycle juggled three fire torches.

Leah was so absorbed in the show that she didn't immediately notice Isabella give a small cry and start scrabbling around by their feet.

"What's wrong," whispered Freya.

"I've dropped my purse, Mum. My pocket money's gone everywhere." Isabella's face crumpled. She looked as though she was about to burst into tears.

Freya sighed, bent down and started picking up the coins, which were scattered all over the floor. Leah stole one last look at the juggling unicyclist and followed suit. Soon they had returned all the money to Isabella's purse and settled back down to watch the rest of the show.

No-one noticed that Oscar had used the diversion to slip out of the tent unseen.

10
Reunited

It was only during the interval that Freya realised her son's seat was empty.

"Where's Oscar?" she asked.

"Gone to the toilet," Isabella said. "He won't be long."

"He's going to miss Lightning if he's not careful," said Leah.

Isabella gave a wicked grin. "Not a chance."

The clowns had reduced the audience to fits of giggles when the ringmaster stepped back into the spotlight.

"And now, ladies and gentlemen, we bring you Lightning the Wonder Horse and his amazing rider Hugo!"

The Cremello stallion burst into the tent and galloped around the ring, his mane and tail flying. Standing on his back with his arms outstretched was a teenage boy in white jodhpurs and a midnight blue sequinned jacket. His blond hair was as fair as Lightning's coat.

A ripple of excitement spread through the big top. Leah clutched her seat and watched in awe as Hugo vaulted on and off the mighty stallion as he thundered around the ring. Lightning's ears flicked back and forth as his young rider swung to a handstand, crossed his legs in mid-air and landed facing the stallion's tail.

Isabella jumped to her feet and started waving frantically. Leah was surprised to see Hugo wink back. He sat for a few strides and then stood again, turned, bent his legs and performed a perfect somersault, landing neatly on Lightning's broad back. Hugo pulled the stallion to a halt in the centre of the ring and squeezed his heels. Lightning reared, his forelegs waving. Hugo clung to his back, one hand wrapped around a chunk of the stallion's mane, his other arm raised in celebration. The audience went wild.

The unicyclist who had been juggling fire torches earlier appeared in the ring, brandishing a torch. He marched over to a big metal hoop that had been lowered from the ceiling, used the torch to light the hoop, gave a flamboyant bow and left.

Leah watched the flames dart and flicker until the whole ring was aflame. Lightning dropped to the floor and Hugo kicked him into a canter. The audience began clapping slowly as the stallion increased his speed to a steady gallop. Hugo turned Lightning towards the ring of fire. Leah was so focused on the Cremello stallion that at first she didn't register the muffled whinny. But when Lightning skidded to a halt in front of the fire hoop she cocked her head and heard a second neigh.

So did Lightning. He stood as still as an ice sculpture, his head high as he sniffed the air. Hugo clicked his tongue and coaxed him forwards. But the stallion refused to move. The clapping fizzled out and someone in the audience jeered. The ringmaster stalked in and cracked his whip. The sound rang out like a gunshot, making Leah jump. But Lightning didn't move a muscle.

And Leah suddenly realised why.

She saw Oscar first. He walked towards Lightning and Hugo with a nervous smile on his face, holding the end of a lead rope.

"What on earth is he doing?" spluttered Freya.

Oscar tweaked the rope and Juno bustled in behind him, her chestnut ears pricked. When she saw Lightning on the other side of the ring of fire she whinnied again. The stallion neighed back, his cream neck arched. Leah stood and peered around her godmother.

"Echo," she breathed, as the palomino colt trotted in by his dam's side, his tiny hooves leaving the faintest imprint on the sandy circus floor. Oscar paused, suddenly uncertain. Hugo slid from Lightning's back and beckoned him closer.

"I can't see!" whined the boy sitting behind Leah. She sat down reluctantly.

Juno walked up to the mighty stallion and nipped him gently on the withers. The audience laughed and she swished her tail haughtily. Lightning bent his head towards Echo and whickered. The foal skittered across to him, allowing the stallion to nuzzle his neck. Above them the fairy lights twinkled brightly.

Leah glanced around her. The audience was transfixed by the scene in front of them. It was so quiet in the big top that you could hear the flames as they crackled around the metal hoop beside the horses. Juno flicked her tail again, sending a tiny spark into the air. It landed on the ground and died away.

But then Leah saw a second spark flutter like a firefly onto the bottom of Juno's tail where it began to smoulder. Her blood ran cold.

11
Fighting Fire

"Fire!" Leah croaked, pointing to Juno.

No-one took any notice.

Leah jumped to her feet, clambered past
Freya and Isabella and raced down to the
entrance to the big top. She grabbed the fire
extinguisher and sprinted back to the ring. She
pulled the pin, aimed the nozzle at Juno's tail
and squeezed the trigger.

The hiss of foam made all three horses
spook. Leah kept the fire extinguisher trained
on Juno's tail. The mare kicked out in fear.
One hoof landed squarely in Leah's stomach
and she dropped the fire extinguisher in
surprise.

The audience roared with laughter. They think it's all part of the act, Leah thought desperately. She darted towards the fire extinguisher. But before she could reach it Hugo had torn his jacket off and wrapped it tightly around Juno's tail, smothering the fire.

Leah sank to her knees in relief. "Thank you," she cried.

"No problem," said Hugo. He turned to Oscar and pointed to the small opening at the far end of the circus ring. "Take these two out and they can spend some more time with Lightning later. Because right now I have a show to finish."

Hugo grabbed a chunk of Lightning's mane and vaulted onto the stallion's back. "Where were we?" he asked the audience.

"You were about to jump through the fire," shouted a girl in the second row. There was a ripple of laughter.

"So we were," Hugo grinned and patted the stallion's neck. "Come on boy, let's show them how it's done."

Hugo kicked the stallion back into a canter and they circled the ring. Hugo's eyes were fixed on the burning hoop. Leah could see his lips moving as he murmured to his horse. She gasped as Hugo jumped to his feet, spun in the air and landed facing Lightning's tail again.

"He's going to jump facing backwards!" she cried.

"Shush!" said the boy sitting behind her.

As Lightning approached the ring of fire everyone held their breath. He tossed his mane and suddenly he was soaring through the flames. Leah was the first to jump out of her seat, clapping wildly, but soon everyone was on their feet, cheering for Hugo and his wonder horse.

All too soon the show was over. The audience trooped out, leaving a trail of popcorn and sweet wrappers. Freya looked at her daughter. "I want to know exactly what's been going on," she said sternly. "No lies - not even white ones." Isabella glanced sheepishly at Leah. "Just tell me what you and Oscar have been up to."

Isabella took a deep breath and told her mum how they must have accidentally left the gate to the orchard open the previous summer, how Juno had escaped and how Hugo had brought her home again.

"Was he angry?" Freya asked.

"No, he thought it was funny," she said.

Freya raised her eyebrows. "And what about this evening?"

"We wanted Echo to meet his dad. It was Leah's idea," Isabella said.

"Pardon?" said Leah.

"Well, not exactly your idea. But you said it was a shame that Echo would never get to meet his dad, which got me thinking, perhaps there was a way."

"So dropping your money was just a diversion so your brother could sneak out and fetch Juno and Echo?" Freya said.

"Yes. Clever wasn't it?" Isabella grinned. "That was definitely my idea."

The girl in the sparkly pink leotard appeared beside them.

"Hugo's ready for you now. Come with me."

They followed her across the sandy circus floor and through the door at the back of the big top. Outside the circus performers had changed back into everyday clothes and were beginning to unhitch guy ropes and dismantle seating.

"Are you going already?" Leah had asked, surprised.

The girl nodded. "First thing tomorrow."

"Must be strange, always being on the move."

"You get used to it."

Isabella saw Oscar and the horses first and raced over to them. Lightning and Juno were standing side by side pulling wisps of hay from a haynet while Echo skittered about between them, clearly having the time of his life.

"He's quite the entertainer, isn't he?" said Hugo. "He definitely takes after his dad."

"Yes," mused Isabella. "I wonder if we should start teaching him some tricks. Get him used to fire now, while he's still young."

Freya shook her head in disbelief. "Don't even think about it."

12

Danger on the Mudflats

The long, lazy days of summer were drawing to a close and Leah knew the misty mornings and darker evenings meant that autumn was just around the corner. She watched wistfully as the trees in the orchard turned russet, ripe apples falling with a thud onto the grass below. When she ran her hands along Juno's neck and felt the mare's coat growing thicker it was an unhappy reminder that her time at Hollow End was almost over. Ahead lay city life and a new school year. No Juno, no Echo. No Freya or the twins. Leah wasn't looking forward to it at all.

She spent every spare minute in the orchard

with Juno and Echo.

"They probably think you're part of their herd," joked Isabella. "You'll be growing a tail and another set of legs if you're not careful."

The last few precious days slipped through her fingers like sand and before she knew it Leah was waking up on her last morning at the farm.

"Are you looking forward to going home?" asked Freya as Leah helped her feed the sheep for the last time.

Leah shook her bucket of sheep pellets and watched as the sheep and their lambs came running. "Not really. I can't wait to see Sparkle. And Mum and Dad of course," she added hastily. "But I'm going to miss everyone here so much."

"You're always welcome, Leah. After all, you are my favourite goddaughter," said Freya.

"I'm your only goddaughter," Leah laughed.

Her parents were due to arrive just after four o'clock. After lunch Leah trudged upstairs to her bedroom to pack. After half-heartedly gathering some clothes from the chest of drawers she sank onto the bed, her heart heavy. She was staring into space when there was a tap at the door.

"It's only us," said Isabella. "We've got something for you."

The twins slipped into her room and Oscar produced a loosely-wrapped parcel from behind his back. "Ta da!"

"It was my idea," said Isabella. "I hope you like it."

"I wanted to dig you up some more worms, but Mum said no," said her brother. "I can't think why."

Leah pulled at the paper. Inside was a carved wooden photo frame. She turned it over to see a photo of Juno and Echo grazing side by side in the sunlit orchard.

She swallowed the lump in her throat. "It's lovely. Thank you."

"We thought it could stand beside your photo of Sparkle," said Isabella.

Leah wrapped the photo in her dressing gown and placed it in her suitcase. Oscar wandered out of the room but Isabella stayed and watched as Leah carelessly slung clothes in her case.

"No-one could call you Miss Neat Freak these days," Isabella remarked.

Leah looked down at her clothes. Her tee-shirt was crumpled and there was a faint grass stain on her shorts from where she'd been lying in the long grass watching Echo prance and leap around the orchard the previous evening. She smiled at the memory. She would rather have grass stains on her shorts and have spent time with the horses than have clean clothes any day.

"Being neat and tidy doesn't seem so important any more," she said.

Packing finished, Leah zipped the case and dropped it onto the floor. "I'm going to say goodbye to Juno and Echo. Do you mind if I go on my own?"

"'Course not. I've got the chickens to feed anyway," said Isabella.

Leah ran down the stairs and out of the back door. She could see her godmother weeding in the kitchen garden and raced over.

"Can I pick a couple of carrots for Juno and Echo?" she asked.

"Of course. Your mum just rang. They're

running a bit late."

Good, thought Leah as she tip-toed between the rows of cabbages and leeks until she reached the carrots. She loosened the soil around a couple and tugged until they came away in her hand. Holding them by their fernlike tops, she headed towards the orchard.

It was a beautiful afternoon and the sun was warm on her back as she leant on the gate and whistled to Juno. Usually the mare ambled straight over looking for a treat, Echo trotting by her side, but today they were nowhere to be seen. Assuming they were snoozing out of sight, Leah whistled again, louder this time. But still they didn't come.

Leah scrambled over the gate, dropping onto the ground with a thud. She began walking towards the far corner of the orchard to the bottom gate that led to the lane. There was still no sign of the mare and foal.

"The gate's shut. They must be here somewhere," she muttered to herself, peering behind tree trunks and even into the branches, as if Juno and Echo had suddenly grown wings and learnt to fly. But the only tree dweller was a willow warbler, who eyed her beadily from his leafy perch.

By the time Leah reached the bottom gate and she still hadn't found the horses her pulse was racing. Feeling light-headed with worry she put her hand on the gate to steady herself. To her horror it swung open. The latch wasn't fastened.

"They must have escaped!" she cried. She looked down at the dusty ground by her feet. There were two sets of hoofprints, one the size of her hand, the other much smaller, leading onto the stony narrow track towards the road. Leah stumbled after them, her heart crashing in her ribcage. She reached the lane and skidded to a halt, hoping Juno and Echo were grazing happily on the verge by the tattered circus poster. But the lane was deserted. Leah looked left and right. Which way would they have gone? Without thinking she turned right towards the river.

"Juno!" puffed Leah as she sprinted down the lane. There was no answering whicker. As she neared the river she called again, bellowing at the top of her voice, "JUNO!"

She stopped in her tracks as a panicky whinny rang out across the mudflats. She set off at a jog, following the lane as it curved towards the river. Around the last bend was the ribbon of grass where she'd daydreamed about Lightning. Leah blinked. There was Juno, standing exactly where she'd stood that afternoon. Only this time she wasn't nibbling the long grass, she was standing stock still, staring out towards the mudflats, her nostrils flared, her flaxen mane rippling in the wind.

Leah followed her gaze. A tiny brown horse was rising from the mudflats like a mythical creature in a fairy tale. She blinked and looked again and realised with cold, hard dread that it wasn't a mythical creature emerging from the mire at all.

It was Echo. And he was stuck fast in the mud.

13
The Rescue

Leah stood rooted to the spot, watching Echo floundering. Every time he struggled to free one of his long legs he sank deeper into the mud. He was panting heavily and Leah could see the whites of his eyes. She called out, forcing herself to sound calm. He turned his mud-covered head towards her and gave a high-pitched whinny.

Echo's call for help spurred Leah into action. She ran to the edge of the mudflats and gingerly took a step forward, testing to see if the mud would hold her weight. It seemed firm, so she took another step towards the foal, and another.

"I'm coming," she called. Echo stopped struggling and watched Leah edge her way towards him.

Just when she thought she would be able to reach the foal she trod on a band of softer sand. Her trainer sank down and almost disappeared altogether. Her godmother's words of warning rang in her ears. Don't go near the mudflats, whatever you do. They're like quicksand. It's so easy to sink down into the mud and get stuck.

Leah faltered. She couldn't bear to leave Echo on his own in the mud. But if she became stuck she wouldn't be able to rescue him anyway. No-one would know where they were, and by the time Freya realised she was missing it might be too late for them both.

She made up her mind. "I'm going for help, Echo. I'll be as quick as I can."

Leah wrenched her foot from the oozing mud, cast a final look at the exhausted foal and raced towards the farm, hoping with all her heart that she'd made the right decision.

Freya was still in the kitchen garden weeding

around the lettuce plants when Leah tore over like a whirlwind. She took one look at her goddaughter's mud-encrusted trainers and jumped to her feet.

"What's happened?"

"It's Echo. He's stuck in the mud," Leah said, brushing a tear from her cheek. "We have to rescue him!"

"Go and find Isabella and Oscar. Tell them we need the ladder. It's leaning up against the side of the barn. I'll get Eric and Joseph. We'll take the tractor down to the river."

Pale-faced, the three children clambered onto the trailer of the tractor. Freya and Joseph stacked the ladder, a dozen long planks of wood and a coil of rope beside them.

"All OK?" shouted Eric over his shoulder. They nodded and he switched on the ignition. The tractor coughed and spluttered into life and began lumbering towards the river.

After what seemed like a decade Eric pulled up on the grass and switched off the engine. Juno was still staring out over the mudflats, her body trembling with fear. Leah shielded her eyes from the sun, frantically scanning the mudflats for Echo.

"I can't see him!" she cried.

"There he is," pointed Oscar. Leah looked again. The foal's legs were almost totally submerged in the mud. His brown eyes were fixed on them. Eric slung the rope around his shoulder and he and Joseph started laying the wooden planks onto the mud, using them as a safe pathway to Echo.

Leah watched, her heart in her mouth, as the two farmhands walked across the planks to the foal. She could hear them murmuring to Echo as they slipped one end of the rope under his belly twice. They secured their makeshift hoist and Joseph ran back along the planks with the other end of the rope and tied it to the back of the trailer.

"Gently does it," he said, nodding to Freya, who jumped behind the wheel and started the engine. She inched the tractor forwards. Leah and the twins watched the rope take up the slack until it was taut. There was a loud squelching noise as Echo was pulled from the mud. Eric gave the thumbs up, lifted the foal onto his burly shoulders and carried him across the planks to the riverbank where he placed him at Juno's feet.

The mare whickered. Echo staggered to his feet and then collapsed in a shivering heap on the ground.

"He's shattered," said Freya. "Let's get him home."

Back at the farm Isabella ran indoors to find blankets while Oscar brought out bucket after bucket of warm water so Leah could rinse the mud from Echo's coat.

"You're palomino again," she told the foal with relief, tipping the last bucket of muddy water into the drain. He nuzzled her hand and she kissed his nose.

Isabella appeared with an armful of blankets and towels. They dried Echo and wrapped a fleece blanket around him, securing it with a couple of Oscar's elasticated belts. Soon he was settled in the stable with his dam. The children watched over the door as his head drooped. Soon he was fast asleep, Juno standing over him like a sentry. Isabella and

Oscar wandered back into the house but Leah stayed where she was, watching Echo as he slept.

Freya found her there half an hour later.

"I've got some good news and some bad news," she said.

"I suppose I'd better have the bad news first," Leah said.

"Your mum and dad have just arrived. It's time to go."

Leah sighed. "And the good news?"

"Their lecture tour was such a success they've been asked to go back next summer. Your mum asked if you could come and stay again. I told her we'd love nothing more. That's if you want to, of course?"

Leah threw her arms around her godmother. "Are you kidding? Of course I would!"

14
Home Again

Leah Lindberg grabbed a pair of jodhpurs and a sweater from the tangle of clothes on her bedroom floor and pulled them on. She rummaged through the clutter on her desk in search of her watch, eventually finding it tucked beneath her pencil case and an old crisp packet. Picking up the photo of Juno and Echo from her bedside table, Leah headed downstairs with a spring in her step.

Her mum was making toast. "Your first day helping out at the stables. Are you looking forward to it?"

"You bet," said Leah, who had been so excited she'd hardly slept a wink. After six

weeks away she couldn't wait to see Sparkle
and the other ponies at the riding school.

Her mum handed her two slices of toast, a
packed lunch and two carrots and soon she
was on her way, splashing through the
puddles on the potholed track to the stables.

"Hey, Leah!" shouted a voice and Leah
turned to see Lisa behind her. She slowed so
the other girl could catch her up.

"Are you here for your riding lesson?"

"No. Even better than that. I'm going to be
helping out every Saturday, too."

"Cool," said Lisa. "Did you have a good
summer?"

"The best," said Leah, reaching in her
rucksack for the photo of Juno and Echo. "I
was wrong, there was a horse at the farm
when I arrived. And then there were two."

Lisa looked puzzled. "What do you mean?"

She listened in astonishment as Leah told
her about Echo and Lightning and the drama
on the mudflats.

"Wow," she said. "It makes my summer
sound really boring."

They arrived at the stables and found Sam in

the office. She handed the two girls a sheet torn from a notebook.

"Here's the list of ponies we need for each lesson. I need them caught, groomed and tacked up so they are ready ten minutes before their lessons are due to start. Do you need me to show you what to do, Leah?"

"No, I'm good thanks. I had plenty of practice in the summer."

Sam smiled approvingly and handed them a headcollar each. "Sparkle and Copper are the first two I need. Lisa'll show you where they are."

They stomped through the mud to the pony paddock. Leah paused at the gate. "It's been so long. I don't suppose he'll recognise me," she said.

But she needn't have worried. When he heard her whistle Sparkle lifted his head, whinnied and trotted over. She offered him a carrot and slipped his headcollar on. "You're absolutely filthy," she said fondly.

They followed Lisa and Copper back through the mud to the yard and Leah tied Sparkle up next to the chestnut gelding.

"This is where the hard work starts," said Lisa.

"It's funny," said Leah. "I used to think that riding was the best bit about horses. But I was wrong."

"What do you mean?"

"I couldn't ride Juno or Echo, but it didn't matter one little bit. I just enjoyed looking after them."

"Even the mucky bits?"

Leah pushed her fringe out of her eyes, wiping a smear of dirt across her forehead as she did. She regarded Sparkle, who was dozing in the autumn sunshine, his coat so caked in mud that he looked dun, not sparkling white, and her heart expanded with love.

She grinned at her new friend and reached for a dandy brush.

"Especially the mucky bits."

The Pony of Tanglewood Farm

1

The New Girl

The first thing Alice Winter noticed about the new girl was her dazzling confidence. It was unusual for someone to start school halfway through the term, and Alice's classmates were staring at her with open curiosity. Alice would
have hated all the attention, but the new girl seemed totally unfazed. She stood at the front of the classroom and smiled widely back at them.

"This is Susanna Thorp," said their teacher, Mrs Johnson, a good-natured woman who was as short as she was round. "Susanna and her family have been living in the States for the last five years and have just moved back. Susanna is joining our class. I hope you'll all make her very welcome."

The second thing Alice noticed about Susanna Thorp was the silver horse brooch she wore on her sweater, just above the embroidered logo of their school. The tiny horse was prancing, its mane and tail flowing and its forelegs waving. Alice imagined the horse sparking into life, and smiled as she pictured him galloping right off the blue and yellow logo, down Susanna's sleeve and away.

Alice loved all animals, but most of all she loved horses. There was something about their beauty, grace and kindness that melted her heart. Alice didn't have her own pony, but once a month her parents paid for her to have a lesson at the local riding school. Alice wished she could have ridden every week but she knew it was all they could afford. She looked forward to that one hour in the saddle all month and, when the day finally arrived, she enjoyed every minute. She usually rode Sandy, a plump chestnut mare with a flaxen mane and tail, who had a nasty habit of stopping dead as they trotted around the menage. More often than not Alice flew

straight over her shoulder and landed on the
floor with a bone-shaking thud, but she never
minded and always hopped straight back on,
desperate not to miss a single second of her
lesson. It was just over three weeks since her
last ride and Alice missed the mischievous
Sandy. But at least she only had to wait
another five days until she could see the mare
again. Alice made a mental note to check her
mum had plenty of carrots in.

Her daydream was interrupted by Mrs
Johnson.

"You'll be sitting next to Alice," the teacher
said, pointing to the empty seat beside her.

Alice's right hand shot to her face, as if it
had a life of its own. She rested her chin in
her palm, her fingers covering her cheek. She
tried to make the gesture look casual, but it
was too late. She watched, resigned, as a look
of shock swept across the new girl's face,
swiftly followed by pity. Shock she was used
to, but even after all this time she still found
people's pity hard to bear.

"Hi Alice," the girl said, flinging her rucksack
under the desk and sliding into her chair. She

had a strong American accent.

"Hello," Alice mumbled back. Her cheek felt hot under her sticky palm and she wondered why she bothered trying to hide her face. Susanna had seen it anyway. Alice forced herself to cross her arms and look at the whiteboard on which Mrs Johnson had written the twelve times table and was trying, without much luck, to get the children to repeat after her.

While she chanted along with the rest of the class Alice knew the new girl would be checking out the scar that ran from her right cheekbone to her mouth in a jagged line. The doctor who'd carefully stitched her torn skin back together had assured her that the blemish would fade in time but, three years later, it was still a livid red against her pale skin.

Alice no longer got a shock when she looked in the mirror. The people who saw her every day, her classmates, the postman, her neighbours, didn't take any notice any more either.

Occasionally a younger child would ask her

what had happened, and she had a ready-made supply of tall stories to tell them. She was trying to tame a wild horse when she was thrown onto a rocky path. She'd been electrocuted by an electric eel while fishing with her granddad. She'd been struck by lightning. The more shocked the child looked, the further Alice stretched the truth. Sometimes she wondered if she gave them nightmares.

Alice could still feel the prickle of Susanna's gaze and she glared at her.

"Don't you know it's rude to stare?" she muttered. The new girl looked away, embarrassed. Alice began chanting again, counting down the hours until the end of school when she could return to Tanglewood Farm, where no-one judged her on her looks. They loved her just as she was.

2

Girl Friday

Alice Winter lived next door to Tanglewood Farm Animal Rescue Centre and, as far as she was concerned, it was the best place in the world to live. Forget castles or stately homes, forget penthouse apartments in towering skyscrapers that skimmed the clouds. Alice loved being next door to the tumbledown farm and the motley collection of animals who called it home.

Every other day new animals turned up, skinny, bedraggled and unloved. The dog warden would drive up in his familiar white van and Alice would watch from the window as he unlocked the rear doors and produced another waif and stray with all the panache of a magician pulling a rabbit out of a hat.

"Where do they all come from?" wondered Alice one day.

"People decide to buy a pet on a whim. They fall in love with the puppies and kittens they see in pet shops and forget they grow old, just like us," said her mum. "They don't want to know when they aren't cute and fluffy any more, and they dump them without a second thought. Luckily for them there is always Julia."

Alice's mum's best friend Julia Hall had inherited Tanglewood when her parents died. The house had been a working farm but, although farming was in their blood, Julia and her eight-year-old son Peter had other plans. Within a few weeks a hand-painted sign, Tanglewood Animal Rescue Centre, had been tacked to the fence outside and people started bringing them the pets no-one else wanted.

Alice's mum had known Julia since they were both toddlers. They had grown up living next door to each other and were as close as sisters. Alice envied their friendship. Although she got on with the girls at school she wasn't particularly close to anyone. All she wanted to talk about was ponies, but they were more interested in clothes and pop songs. They didn't have much in common.

Alice spent almost as much time at Tanglewood as she did at home. She helped Julia feed the animals and clean out their runs. She and Peter groomed the cats and threw endless balls for the dogs. Together they spent hours gaining the trust of the most timid animals. Animals like Milo, a scrawny golden cocker spaniel who had arrived at the rescue centre quivering with fear, so terrified that he wouldn't venture out of his kennel. Alice and Peter had taken it in turns to station themselves on a cushion outside and had talked nonsense to him for days until he'd finally tottered out and given Peter's hand a cautious sniff. Since that breakthrough Milo was becoming braver by the minute.

Julia called Alice her Girl Friday and Alice was only too happy to help. Alice preferred animals to humans. There was no contest. Animals were trusting, kind and friendly.

Animals didn't judge you or the way you looked. They didn't worry about crooked noses, wonky eyes or scars that ran across your cheek. If you treated them well, they would repay you with love and devotion.

"Good day?" asked her mum as they accelerated away from school. It was raining and Alice watched the windscreen wipers as they swept back and forth.

"It was OK. A new girl started. Susanna something."

"Oh yes, I met her mum in the playground. Mrs Thorp. They've moved into that big house next to the river. Did you like her?"

"Not sure yet. I'll let you know when I decide," Alice answered, running her index finger down her scar absentmindedly.

An old horse lorry pulled out in front of them. The road was too narrow to overtake so Alice's mum changed into a lower gear and they followed the lorry as it lumbered around the windy lanes. They watched, surprised, when the driver indicated left and turned into their road. Julia was standing at the end of her drive waving her arms at the lorry. The driver pulled over and jumped out of the cab. Alice sprinted over to Julia.

"More llamas?" she asked.

Julia smiled. "Not this time, no. Why don't you go and have a look."

The driver lowered the ramp. Alice dropped her rucksack onto the wet concrete and walked slowly up the ramp. The rain was drumming down now and her hair and school jumper were soaked. She brushed a strand of wet hair from her eyes and gazed into the back of the lorry.

Her eyes widened. Standing huddled against the far partition was a pony. He was so thin his ribs stood out like the wooden bars of a xylophone. His head was low and he was swaying slightly, as if it was sapping all his energy and concentration just to remain standing.

Alice blinked. When she opened her eyes the pony was still there. He had turned his head and was looking at her. His dull, matted coat was as black as midnight. Between his eyes a small white star blazed brightly.

3
Midnight Star

Alice stared at the pony. He wobbled
dangerously and for one terrifying moment
she thought he was going to collapse. She
darted forward and leaned against him,
propping him up. He turned his head and
nudged her gently. Alice ran her hand down
his bony neck. Her fingers met bare skin. She
saw something she hadn't noticed before - a
scar that ran across the pony's shoulder in the
shape of a crescent moon.

"Who did this to you?" she said softly. She
looked into his sad brown eyes but there was
no answer there.

She felt Julia's arm around her. "He was

found tethered to a tree on that patch of wasteland behind the industrial estate," Julia told her. "Someone found him this morning. He'd been there without food or water for days."

"You don't normally take ponies," said Alice's mum.

"I know," said Julia, untying the pony's leadrope. "I haven't really got the space. But I couldn't say no to this one. He's in a terrible state. He's skin and bone and his legs are covered in sores. I'm not sure he'll survive the night."

Occasionally animals at Tanglewood died of old age or illness, despite the care Julia, Alice and Peter lavished on them. They were buried in the top paddock, in the shade of a horse chestnut tree. Alice always placed a small wooden cross in the soil to mark their grave. Although she mourned the loss of every animal, over the years she'd learnt to accept death as part of life. But the thought of this pony not making it made her feel sick to the pit of her stomach.

"Can't you call the vet?" she asked.

"I already have. He'll be here in an hour or so. Hopefully we'll know more then. Come on, let's get him into the barn and see if he wants something to eat."

As they led the pony slowly down the ramp Alice said, "What are we going to call him?"

"I don't know. Any ideas?"

The name popped into Alice's head unbidden. "Midnight Star," she said. "Star for short."

Julia nodded. Alice's mum looked anxious.

"Don't get too attached to him, Alice. He's very weak. He may not pull through."

"Oh, he will," said Alice with conviction. She opened the barn doors and smiled at them. "I'll make sure he does."

Alice helped settle Star in the barn and gave him a bucket of water and some of the llamas' hay. He sniffed the bucket and turned away.

"You have to drink, little one. Here, try this." She dipped her hands in the water and offered the pony her cupped palms. He sniffed again and drank, his whiskers tickling her fingers. "There's a good boy," she told him. "Have some more."

He drank the water, a handful at a time, and tugged half-heartedly at the hay Alice offered him.

He barely had the strength to turn his head when the barn doors creaked open, but Alice felt his breathing quicken. Peter peered in, his eyes wide.

Alice caressed Star's neck. "It's only Peter. He won't hurt you," she whispered.

Peter edged his way over to them, not wanting to spook the pony. "Hello Star. Hello Alice. Mum sent me to tell you the vet's here."

Alice chewed her lip as the vet listened to Star's heart, checked the pony's teeth and eyes and inspected the sores on his legs.

"He's in a pretty bad way. But his heart rate is normal. I'll rasp his teeth, worm him and work out a treatment plan. He needs feeding up and those sores need dressing every day. With the right care I think he should be fine."

"How old is he?" Alice asked.

"About nine, I should think," said the vet.

Alice scratched Star's poll and smiled. "Same age as me."

Despite the vet's assurances Alice spent a restless night dreaming about Star. Towards dawn she woke to the sound of gulls squawking overhead. She pulled on jeans and a sweater, ran downstairs and let herself out of the back door. The sun was rising behind the barn, turning the sky orange. Alice heaved open the barn doors and stared into the gloom. Star was lying in the straw, as still as a stone statue. Her heart pounding, Alice edged over to him, crouched down and stroked his neck, her head cocked as she listened. His breathing was slow and steady and she felt dizzy with relief. He stirred, opened one eye and whickered. Suddenly she knew that he was going to be OK.

4

A Chance Meeting

Over the next few weeks Alice spent every spare second with Star. She groomed the pony for hours and took him for walks to strengthen his weakened muscles. After breakfast she would select the best carrots from the vegetable rack at home and run over to the farm to give them to him. After school she led him to the places where the greenest grass grew. Peter and Milo often came with them to keep them company. Her dad was baffled to find the four of them in the middle of his beautifully-manicured lawn one day. They looked so happy together, relaxing in the sun, that he didn't have the heart to tell Alice off.

Slowly they all began to notice tiny changes. One by one Star's ribs disappeared. The sores on his legs healed. His quarters started to round out and his neck no longer looked hollow. His ebony coat gleamed in the summer sun and his eyes, once so sad, began to sparkle. Alice taught him to shake a hoof and take a bow. She even managed to teach him to play football and he would push the ball about with his nose for hours.

When the vet arrived eight weeks later he couldn't believe the transformation. And when Star held out a hoof for him to shake he shook his head in amazement.

"I can't believe it's the same pony," he said.

"It just goes to show what a bit of love can do. But I can't take the credit. It's all down to Alice," said Julia.

"Well, keep up the good work. I'd say he'll be strong enough to ride in a couple of weeks."

Alice looked at Julia, her eyes shining. Julia smiled back.

"At least I don't have to look far for a

jockey."

Star dominated Alice's thoughts when she was awake and crept into her dreams when she was asleep. She was so preoccupied with the little black gelding that she completely forgot about her monthly riding lesson until her mum reminded her at breakfast the following day.

She walked up the track to the riding stables, her hat under her arm and a carrot for Sandy in her pocket. Her lesson was about to start and she hurried over to Sandy's stable. As she led the chestnut mare to the mounting block she heard a familiar voice.

"Hi Alice!"

Alice turned to see Susanna Thorp sitting astride Sky, a spirited grey gelding who was only given to the more experienced riders. And that didn't include Alice.

"Oh, hello," Alice said, checking Sandy's girth and swinging into the saddle. Susanna joined her as they headed for the menage.

"This is amazing! You didn't tell me you rode."

Alice shrugged. "I only have a lesson once a month." Twelve hours in the saddle a year, out of a possible eight thousand, seven hundred and sixty hours. It didn't sound much when you put it like that.

"I learnt in the States," said Susanna. "My mum and I used to go trail riding every weekend. We rode Western there so I'm just getting used to an English saddle and bridle. I've started having lessons every Saturday."

Lucky you, thought Alice. She studied her classmate. Susanna's cream jodhpurs and black leather jodhpur boots looked expensive and she rode with an easy confidence. Although she had only been at their school for a couple of months Susanna was already one of the most popular girls in their class. She was bubbly and outgoing and all the girls wanted to be her best friend. She always invited Alice to join their playground games but each time Alice said no. She knew Susanna was only including her out of pity. Anyway, she was happy on her own, daydreaming about Star.

They walked around the menage with the

other riders. Alice soon forgot about Susanna and concentrated on sitting tall in the saddle with her heels down, her hands still and her eyes looking straight ahead.

It was great to be riding again and the lesson sped by. For once Sandy was the model pony, listening to Alice's aids and trotting and cantering obediently around the school.

"You're a great rider," said Susanna, as they led the ponies back to the stables at the end of the lesson.

Alice shrugged off the compliment. "Not really, but thanks anyway."

Susanna tied Sky up next to Sandy and the two girls untacked their ponies.

"I rode a beautiful Quarter Horse in the States. She was called Dream. I miss her like crazy," said Susanna. Her face, usually so smiley, was forlorn.

Alice rummaged around for something sympathetic to say.

"Oh, I'm sorry."

"Don't be. It's not your fault." Susanna paused. "Hey Alice, I was wondering, would you like to come to my house after school one day next week?"

Alice was about to say no when she realised that actually she would. She nodded. "Alright. That would be nice."

Susanna looked pleased. "Awesome."

5

A Perfect Fit

On Sunday morning Alice was feeding the
llamas when Julia beckoned her into the barn.

"I've got something to show you," she said,
looking pleased with herself.

Resting on an upturned bale of hay was a
black leather saddle with a spotless white
numnah. A matching snaffle bridle was
hooked over the cantle of the saddle.

"I remembered that my cousin used to have
a pony about Star's size so I gave her a call to
see if she still had his tack. Luckily for us she
did. The leather was a bit stiff so I spent last
night giving it a clean. Looks pretty good,
don't you think?"

Alice beamed. "It looks amazing. Can we see if it fits?"

She grabbed Star's headcollar and a handful of pony nuts and crossed the farmyard to his paddock, Milo at her heels. The pony was dozing in the far corner and she leant on the gate, watching him. He was resting a hind leg and his tail swished occasionally to flick away flies. Alice called softly and when he opened his eyes and saw her he cantered over. As she slipped on his headcollar he shook his hoof for the handful of pony nuts. Alice giggled. He was such a cheeky boy.

After she'd brushed all the mud from his coat, tackled the knots in his mane and tail and picked out his feet, Julia handed her the saddle.

"Take it slowly. I'm guessing he has been ridden in the past, but I don't suppose he's had a saddle on his back for some time," she told Alice.

Star's eyes were full of trust as Alice showed him the saddle. He stood calmly as she placed it on his back as gently as she could, and tightened his girth. Alice picked up the bridle, slipped the reins over his head and, holding the bit with her left hand, brought it up to his mouth, as she'd been taught to do at the riding stables. Star accepted the bit immediately and she passed the headpiece over his ears. Once she'd fastened the noseband and throat lash she stood back and admired him. The black leather tack and brilliant white numnah suited the jet black pony and Alice itched to pull down the stirrups and jump into the saddle.

"He's an old hand at all this," said Julia.

Alice nodded. Her face was full of longing and Julia smiled.

"I know the two weeks end tomorrow but I don't suppose one day is going to make a difference. Go on, go and get your hat. I'll wait with him."

Alice whooped and raced next door. She grabbed her hat from the hallway and sprinted back. Julia laughed. "That was quicker than lightning. Check his girth and I'll give you a leg up. I'd better lead him today to see how he is."

Alice landed lightly in the saddle and her feet

found the stirrups. Star didn't flinch. She gathered up the reins and gave Julia a nervous smile.

"Ready?" Julia asked.

Alice nodded. Julia clipped the leadrope to Star's bit, Alice squeezed with her heels and they set off at a walk, Star's neat, black ears pricked.

Alice had ridden many different ponies at the riding stables over the years. Bay ponies, grey ponies, skewbald ponies and roan ponies. Lazy ponies who were as round as a barrel. Nervous ponies who shied at their own shadow. The minute she sat on Star's back the other ponies were forgotten. She was in paradise.

"Follow me," commanded Susanna. Alice tagged after her as she ran up the stairs, two at a time. When they reached the landing Alice expected Susanna to peel off into one of the many open doors. Instead, she disappeared around a corner and up a second flight of stairs.

Leading off the tiny landing at the top of the

narrow staircase was a single door. Susanna threw it open and beckoned Alice inside.

"My room," she said.

Alice gazed around her. It was a long, narrow room built into the eaves. The walls were whitewashed and covered in pony posters. Light flooded in from a large window on the back wall.

"It's a great room," she said. "Like a writer's garret. Or Rapunzel's tower."

"Thanks. Mum let me choose. We moved about a lot in the States because of Dad's work. I'm so pleased we're going to be staying here for good."

"Must be hard, always being the new girl. I'd hate it," said Alice, rubbing her cheek.

"You get used to it. I was four when we moved to America so it's the only life I've known." She paused. "Alice?"

"Mmm?"

"I hope you don't mind me asking, but how did you get your scar?"

6

The Story of a Scar

Alice was silent. She knew it was only natural that people were curious. She would be too, in Susanna's shoes.

"Sorry, you don't have to tell me. It's none of my business."

"No, it's OK. I don't mind you asking. But it's not very exciting. I ran in front of a swing when I was six. Someone's boot caught me in the cheek and I had to have eighteen stitches."

"Why do you try to hide it?"

Alice looked at her reflection in the mirror above Susanna's dressing table. She would have given anything to have flawless skin. "Wouldn't you?"

Susanna shook her head. "You should be proud of your face. You look like a warrior, an adventurer. It makes you different from everyone else."

"I don't want to be different!"

"Different is a good thing, Alice," Susanna said. "Who wants to be like everyone else? I don't."

As Alice considered this she picked up a photo from Susanna's bedside table. It showed a chestnut pony with a wide blaze, a flaxen mane and tail and kind eyes.

"That's Dream. The pony I had on loan in the States. We had to give her back when we moved. It broke my heart." Susanna's eyes filled with tears.

"She's beautiful. Exactly the same colour as Sandy," Alice said. She could see why Susanna missed the mare so much. She pictured life without Star and shuddered.

"Dream has gone to another loan home now. I don't suppose I'll ever see her again."

Alice replaced the photo and wandered over to the window. The Thorp's large lawn was bordered by a post and rail fence. Beyond the fence was a large paddock in which stood a weather-boarded field shelter and a stable.

"Do your neighbours have horses?" Alice asked.

"No. That field came with the house."

"You could get another pony."

"Believe me, I'm working on it. Though I'm not having much luck at the moment. Mum and Dad say I should be grateful for riding lessons once a week." Susanna remembered that Alice only had one lesson a month. "Sorry Alice. I know you don't get a chance to ride as often as that. You must think I'm spoilt."

"Actually, I'm riding every day at the moment," said Alice.

"At the stables? I haven't seen you there."

"No, at home. Well, next door really."

Susanna looked puzzled. "Next door?"

Alice told Susanna about Tanglewood and the day Star had turned up, all skin and bone. "We've spent the last couple of months feeding him up and last week I started riding him. He's amazing."

Alice hugged herself. She'd had her first

canter on Star the evening before and it had been bliss. She was surprised to see Susanna frowning. "What's wrong?"

"Aren't you worried?"

"What do you mean?"

Susanna backtracked. She liked Alice a lot and didn't want to upset her. "Nothing. Ignore me."

"No, tell me what you mean."

Susanna glanced at the photo on her bedside table and sighed. "He doesn't belong to you, does he? One day he'll be re-homed and you'll never see him again. Just like me and Dream."

Alice was silent. Her thoughts had been so focused on Star getting better that she hadn't considered the future. Of course Star would be re-homed. All the animals at Tanglewood were, once they had been nursed back to full strength.

"Why can't we keep them, Julia?" a seven-year-old Alice had wept, when she'd had to say goodbye to a litter of kittens she'd helped hand rear.

"We must try and re-home every single animal we can, Alice. Otherwise we'll have no room for all the other animals needing our help. It's for the best," Julia had replied.

Over the years both Alice and Peter had learned to be strong. They missed all the animals, some more than others, but there was always a steady stream of newcomers needing their attention. And they knew that they all went to good homes. Everyone wanting to take in a Tanglewood animal was vetted by Julia and, if they didn't meet her very strict criteria, were sent home empty-handed. This didn't happen very often - the people who came to the rescue centre did so because they loved animals and wanted to give an unwanted pet a home for life, no matter how old or scruffy. They weren't interested in posh pedigrees.

People would be falling over themselves to give Star a home. Of course they would. He was the perfect pony.

Alice realised Susanna was watching her, her eyes dark with sympathy.

"You OK?" she asked.

Alice sat on Susanna's bed, hugging her knees, and tried to answer. But the aching lump in her throat made it impossible to speak.

.

7

Practice Makes Perfect

Alice made a decision that night as she lay in bed, fighting tears. She would not ask Julia if she was going to find Star a new home. What if Julia was planning to keep him? After all, Star was in great shape yet Julia hadn't given even the faintest hint that he was to be re-homed. Alice might plant the seed in her mind by asking. Instead she decided to ignore the threat, hoping it would go away.

As summer turned into autumn Alice rode Star every day, gradually building up his fitness. The farrier came and shod him and they explored the lanes and tracks around Tanglewood together. Peter often walked with her, Milo trotting by his side. The spaniel's golden coat was as soft as silk and his brown eyes sparkled with health.

"Do you remember how skinny Milo was when he arrived?" said Peter one day, as they watched the spaniel carry an old shoe up to Star and drop it in front of the bemused pony's nose.

There was no mistaking the pride in his voice. Alice looked at him in concern. His hair was the colour of straw and just as untidy. A scattering of freckles peppered his nose. He was the closest thing to a brother she had.

"You mustn't get too attached," she reminded him.

"I know." His face was woebegone. "Mum says he'll be ready to be re-homed soon."

Alice squeezed his hand. "Maybe she'll let you keep him."

But Peter shook his head. "It's OK, Alice. I know he'll go to a nice home. And there'll be others to take his place, won't there? Animals who need us to look after them."

Alice smiled. "Yes, there are always plenty of animals."

At school her friendship with Susanna grew, and their lunch-hours flew by as they talked non-stop about ponies. Susanna hadn't mentioned Star being re-homed since that day in her bedroom, and it was a subject they both steered well clear of.

Alice was sitting on the steps outside their classroom one Tuesday morning when Susanna saw her and tore over.

"Guess what! The riding school's holding a show at the end of the month. They're renting out the ponies for it. Mum says I can ride Sky in a couple of classes. I'm so excited! And I've had a brilliant idea. Why don't you bring Star?"

"But I've never ridden in a show before. I won't know what to do," said Alice.

"Don't worry. We can learn together."

Alice could already feel butterflies flapping around in her stomach. She touched her scar. She hated people looking at her. But she was so proud of Star. She'd love to show him off to everyone.

Susanna grinned at her. "Come on. It'll be fun."

"Alright. I'll ask Julia."

Alice wasn't sure if she was relieved or horrified when Julia beamed and told her what an excellent idea it was.

She stopped sweeping the yard and scanned the schedule Alice had given her. "Why don't you enter First Ridden and Best Turned Out?'

Alice loved grooming Star until his black coat shone. "OK, we'll do Best Turned Out. But I'm not sure about First Ridden. I don't know what you're supposed to do."

Julia had left her glasses on the kitchen table and squinted as she read the schedule. "Let's see...'First Ridden ponies will walk and trot as a class. After they have been called into line they will be asked to give an individual show, to include walk, trot and canter on both reins, finishing with a halt.' There you go, it'll be a doddle."

The butterflies re-appeared. "I don't know," said Alice. "What if I fall off in front of everyone?"

"I tell you what," said Julia. "Let's ask Star what he thinks." They walked over to Star's stable. Alice called him and he stuck his head over the stable door. "What d'you reckon Midnight Star. Want a chance to shine?"

The pony whickered and they both laughed.

Alice held up her hands. "OK, we'll do it. But only if you promise to help."

They practised a short show in the paddock behind the farmhouse, watched by Julia, Peter, Milo and a couple of llamas. Alice walked, trotted and cantered Star on the left leg, then changed legs at a trot on the diagonal and repeated the paces on the right rein. Alice eased him from a canter to a trot and then sat deeply in the saddle for a few strides before she squeezed the reins to bring him back into a walk. Julia was smiling.

"I don't know what you were worried about. That was fantastic. You were both balanced and relaxed and the transitions were lovely and smooth."

Alice ran a hand down Star's neck. "I suppose we've still got plenty of time to practice."

"Don't do the show over and over,

otherwise Star will learn it off by heart and he'll start anticipating the transitions before you ask him. Run through it in your head as many times as you like, but you should only practice it a couple of times. "

Alice began counting down the days to the horse show with a curious mix of terror and excitement.

"It's sixteen days away. That's three hundred and eighty four hours. Or twenty three thousand and forty minutes," she told Susanna one lunchtime.

Susanna laughed. She was entering Handy Pony and one of the novice jumping classes on Sky and wasn't nervous at all. Alice couldn't understand it.

"OK, so how many seconds is that?"

"One million, three hundred and eighty two thousand and four hundred," Alice chirruped.

Susanna raised an eyebrow. "Did you just do that sum in your head?"

Alice giggled. "No, I worked it out on Dad's calculator this morning. It's not long though, is it? Think of all those seconds that have already vanished into thin air since we've been talking. Anyway, I've worked out a way of remembering our show without Star practising it too often. I've been walking, trotting and cantering around his field while he watches. He thinks I'm bonkers, but at least I should be able to remember what to do."

8

The Day of the Show

One by one the seconds, minutes and hours Alice had been counting so carefully slipped through her fingers and the day of the show dawned. She was awake with the songbirds, her stomach churning. Julia's cousin had lent her a pair of cream breeches, a white shirt and stock and a black show jacket. They were a bit old-fashioned and slightly too big but were in mint condition. Alice brushed a speck of lint from the sleeve of the jacket as she headed out of her room and down the stairs.

Star was grazing in the far corner of his field. Alice vaulted over the gate and called. He lifted his head and whinnied. She held out a carrot and he trotted over, his ears pricked and his brown eyes inquisitive. The carrot disappeared with a crunch and he nudged her pockets in search of more treats. Alice scratched his poll and regarded him. When he'd arrived at Tanglewood his black coat had been matted and dull and he'd been so weak he'd hardly been able to stand. Now his coat was sleek and he was strong and healthy. She knew how proud she would be, riding this pony in front of everyone at the show. Suddenly the butterflies vanished and she grinned. It was going to be fun.

She heard a latch open and looked up to see Peter waving from his bedroom window.

"Need any help?" he called softly, not wanting to wake his mum.

Alice nodded and he was down in a flash, still wearing his pyjamas with his hair rumpled. They spent the next hour washing Star from head to foot. The little back gelding stood patiently as Peter brushed out his tail and Alice combed his mane and oiled his hooves. By the time Julia appeared, her hands curled around a mug of coffee, Star was gleaming from head to foot.

"He looks a million dollars."

Alice chewed her bottom lip. "I read in my pony magazine that he should really be plaited for Best Turned Out."

"Wait there." Julia disappeared into the kitchen and re-appeared a few minutes later with an old ice-cream tub filled with tiny rubber bands, a thick darning needle, black thread and a small pair of scissors.

"Using rubber bands is quicker, but it's not so neat. I think we'll use a needle and thread today," she said.

Julia dampened Star's mane and divided it into nine sections, fastening each with an elastic band to keep them in place. Starting with the section nearest Star's head, she slid off the elastic band, divided the mane into three and began plaiting.

"You need to plait it tightly, otherwise it'll work loose and end up looking like a dog's dinner," mumbled Julia through a mouthful o darning needle and thread.

"How do you know all this?" asked Alice, watching Julia sew around the end of the plait to secure it. She folded the plait in half by turning the end under, then folded it in half again and stitched through it several times until it was secure.

"My cousin used to compete a lot when she was younger and I often used to go along for the ride. I wasn't much older than you. She's five years older than me and I suppose I was a bit in awe of her. I was happy to fetch and carry for her, anyway. I also learnt a lot. I thought I'd forgotten, but it's funny how it all comes back to you. Here, you try the next one."

Alice stood on an upturned bucket and started plaiting the next section of Star's mane as tightly as she could. Suddenly she was all fingers and thumbs. Star turned his head and gave her a friendly nudge, knocking her hands so the plait came loose. She blew her fringe out of her eyes and tried again.

"Keep your thumbs on top. It'll help keep the plait nice and tight," Julia advised. This time the plaited length looked almost as neat as Julia's and Alice sewed it through before it had a chance to unravel.

"Good work," said Julia. "You finish his mane and I'll see if I can remember how to do tails."

Half an hour later Star's mane and tail were both plaited. Alice gave his coat a final brush with the body brush.

"What about a quarter mark?" asked Julia.

"That would be great, but I don't know how to do it."

"I think I remember." Julia took the body brush, dampened it in a bucket of water and used it to smooth the hair on Star's rump. She scratched her chin. "I need one of the cats' flea combs. Peter, be a love and go and find me one, please."

Peter darted into the kitchen and came back with a flea comb in his hand. Julia used it against the direction of Star's hair to draw a chequer-board design. She stood back to admire her handiwork. "What d'you reckon?"

"He looks amazing," said Peter. The butterflies in Alice's stomach were back, swooping and leaping uncomfortably, and when she held out her hands she wasn't surprised to see them trembling. She tried to picture riding Star into the show ring but her mind had gone completely blank.

"I can't remember what to do!" she cried.

9

A Red Rosette

Julia smiled. "You'll be fine when you get there. Don't worry." She looked at her watch. "We'd better make a move. You go and get changed while I tack Star up."

It was only a twenty minute hack to the riding school and Alice's mum, Julia and Peter walked with them, carrying a picnic lunch, spare grooming kit and a couple of camping chairs.

The riding school was always busy on a Saturday morning but today it was buzzing. A small paddock behind the stable block was crammed with lorries and trailers. People must have travelled from far afield to compete. Susanna had told Alice that all the riding school ponies were taking part in different classes. As she scanned the yard for her friend Alice saw Sandy tied up outside her stable. The mare was tugging greedily from a haynet, her mane and tail neatly brushed and her chestnut coat glossy. Alice stroked Star's neck, trying to avoid his plaits. His ears were pricked and his stride was bouncy as he looked avidly around him, taking everything in.

"I'll go and see when your first class is," said Julia, melting into the crowds. Alice's mum set down the camping chairs and noticed her daughter's pale face.

"Don't be nervous. It's just a bit of fun. Oh look, there's Susanna. Why don't you go and say hello."

Alice clicked her tongue and trotted over to where Susanna and Sky were standing watching the gymkhana games.

"Alice! There you are! I was worried you'd got cold feet." She slid off Sky and stroked Star's nose. "And you must be the famous Midnight Star. You're right, Alice, he is absolutely beautiful. You are so lucky."

Star held out his near foreleg for Susanna to shake and she laughed. "Beautiful and clever. Can you do any more tricks, lovely Star?"

Alice touched Star's shoulder and he bowed down low. Susanna shrieked with glee. "Don't tell me, can he walk a tightrope too?" she asked.

"We're still working on that," grinned Alice. "Have you had any classes yet?"

Susanna sighed. "We made a show of ourselves in Handy Pony. We managed to open and shut the gate alright but Sky shied when we walked under the washing line and I ended up with a pair of trousers around my neck."

"You got sixth place though," said Alice, noticing a purple rosette on Sky's browband.

"There were only six of us in the class!" giggled Susanna, who didn't seem to mind coming last at all. She stroked Star's nose one last time and jumped back on Sky.

"I'd better go and warm up for the jumping. Good luck and I'll see you later."

Before she knew it, Alice was waiting to ride into the ring for Best Turned Out. There were twelve ponies in the class, and they all looked spotless. She didn't notice the admiring glances all the riders were giving her and Star. The little black pony was turning heads. He walked with an extra bounce in his step, loving all the attention.

The steward called them in and they started walking around the show ring as the judge stood in the middle and watched them. Once they had circled her a couple of times she called them into line. Star stood patiently as the judge worked her way along the line, her hands clasped behind her back and her face inscrutable as she inspected ponies, riders and tack.

"Crikey, she's thorough," said a teenage girl on an immaculate dark bay pony next to Alice. The judge had finished peering into a palomino mare's ears and was now examining the underside of her rider's jodhpur boots.

"I knew there was something I'd forgotten," groaned the girl to Alice's right, twisting her own riding boots and eying the dust underneath balefully. Alice patted Star. Her mum had given her boots a final wipe so fingers crossed she'd pass the clean boots test at least.

Finally it was their turn and the judge gave Star a brisk pat. Was it possible to sit neatly, Alice wondered, as the judge walked up and down Star's sides, scrutinising every inch of the pony and rider. When she felt her face going puce Alice realised she was holding her breath. She exhaled loudly and the judge looked up, her eyebrows raised.

"Sorry. I'm a bit nervous. It's my first ever show," whispered Alice.

To her surprise the judge winked at her. "No reason to be nervous, dear. You've done a terrific job."

Soon the military-style inspection was over and the steward appeared at the judge's side with a small silver trophy and an armful of rosettes. The judge took the cup and red rosette and began striding towards Alice's end of the line. Alice looked behind her, wondering who had won. It must be the girl on the dark bay. The girl obviously thought so

- she was patting her pony's neck and smiling.

But the judge stopped in front of Alice, winked again and, to her utter amazement, handed her the cup and red rosette.

"Congratulations. I couldn't spot a single speck of dust or dirt. And your plaits were faultless. Very impressive for a first show."

Speechless, Alice could only nod her thanks and watch, amazed, as the judge handed out the rest of the rosettes. She would have stayed in line for the rest of the day had the judge not held out her hand signalling her to lead the lap of honour. Star didn't need asking twice and set off at a lively canter. The little black gelding seemed to understand the applause was for him and he arched his neck proudly.

Her mum, Julia and Peter were waiting outside and showered Star with pats.

"Brilliant!" said her mum. "Your first rosette!"

"There'll be plenty of time to celebrate later. First Ridden's the next class," Julia said.

Alice's flushed cheeks drained of colour. Her success was forgotten as fear clawed her chest.

Reading her mind, her mum gave her knee a gentle squeeze. "There's nothing to be worried about. You know your show off by heart. And look at Star. He's having the time of his life."

It was true. His head was bobbing this way and that, taking everything in. In a far field Alice could see ponies thundering up and down a line of bending poles. A girl was urging her piebald cob around a small course of show jumps in the menage Alice usually had her lessons in. Riders were cantering over warm up jumps in the collecting ring. Alice spied Susanna, who was popping Sky over a cross pole. She waved, and stuck her thumb up, wishing her luck. Susanna waved back.

Star was becoming restless and Alice gathered her reins. "Come on. Let's get this over and done with," she told him, and followed the other riders into the ring.

10
Different is Good

Alice found herself sandwiched between a boy on a strawberry roan gelding and a girl on a dappled grey mare. This time the judge was a man dressed in a tweed hacking jacket and dark green corduroys. There were eight ponies and riders in the class and they walked and trotted around the ring until they were told to line up. Star's ears were pricked and he stood quietly as the others completed their individual shows. Alice could feel her nerves stretching tighter and tighter. When their turn finally arrived she gave Star a pat and squeezed her legs. He moved smoothly into his familiar, bouncy walk, his black ears pointing forwards.

Suddenly Alice was back at Tanglewood, walking around Star's paddock trying to memorise their show, the little black pony watching her with curiosity. Walk away on the left rein, then ask for a trot. Remember the correct diagonal! Alice sneaked a look down to Star's shoulder to check she was sitting when Star's near foreleg touched the ground. Ask for a canter. Star struck off on the wrong leg and Alice pulled him back to a trot. After a couple of strides she sat down in the saddle again, remembering to move her outside leg behind the girth when she asked him to canter. This time he cantered on the correct leg and Alice sat deeply in the saddle and kept her back tall and her eyes ahead.

"Sorry Star," she whispered. He flicked an ear back at the sound of her voice.

Make your transition from canter to trot nice and smooth. She increased her feel on the reins and asked him to trot. Remember to change the diagonal when you change reins. Alice sat for two strides as they trotted across the ring.

As they repeated their paces on the right rein Alice finally felt herself relax and, to her surprise, found she was enjoying herself. All too soon she was re-joining the line of ponies, their show over. The judge strode up and down, handing out rosettes. First place to a flashy chestnut pony that Alice didn't recognise, second and third to two ponies from the riding school. The judge had turned on his heels and was making a beeline for Star, a green rosette in his gloved hand. Fourth place!

"Well done," said the judge, attaching the rosette to Star's browband.

"I thought I'd ruined it when we cantered on the wrong leg," said Alice.

"Quite the opposite. You kept a cool head when you made a mistake and corrected it quickly. Well done."

When they came out of the ring Julia was standing next to a man with a camera.

"He's a photographer from the local paper. He wants to take a picture of you both. I mentioned the fact that Star was a rescue pony and he said it would make a nice story."

Alice leapt out of the saddle. "I don't want my picture taken!" she cried, her hand flying to her face. "Peter can do it."

"But you're the one who's nursed Star back to health," Peter pointed out. "Why won't you do it?"

"Why do you think?" Alice demanded.

Peter looked mystified.

"My scar," she hissed.

"Your scar? What's that got to do with anything?"

"Are you crazy?" said Alice, her voice rising to a screech.

Peter shrugged. He'd have thought Alice would have jumped at the chance to be in the paper. Sometimes girls were impossible to fathom.

The photographer cleared his throat. "Right, have we decided who's going to be in the picture?"

Alice's mum stepped forward, lifted her daughter's chin and looked her squarely in the eye.

"I hate to see you hiding behind your scar, Alice. It's part of who you are. You have a lovely face, and that's what people notice, not a bit of scar tissue. Be brave," she said softly.

Alice stroked Star's neck, her hand trailing down to his shoulder. She traced his crescent-shaped scar with her finger. She loved everything about Star, including his scar. It was part of his story. Some might see it as an imperfection, but he would always be perfect in her eyes.

She remembered what Susanna had said, the day she had told her about the accident. How Susanna saw her scar as a clue to unravel, a hint of an interesting story, a badge of honour. Something that singled her out from everyone else, made her different. And different was good, right? Perhaps it was time to accept the way she looked. To be proud of her scar.

She took a deep breath. "OK, I'll do it."

11
The Worst News

Alice was drawing intricate patterns on the dusty floor of the playground with a twig when Susanna ran up, a huge grin on her face.

"Guess what!" she cried, flinging herself down beside Alice.

"I don't know. Give me a clue."

"No time for clues," Susanna said impatiently. "Mum and Dad have finally agreed that I can have a pony!"

"That's fantastic!" said Alice, pleased for her friend.

"I know, I'm so excited," Susanna laughed. A thought struck her. "We'll be able to go riding together!"

Alice imagined them exploring tracks and bridleways on their ponies. It would be fun. "Cool. How soon will you get one?"

"Dad's already started looking, so fingers crossed it won't be long." Susanna hugged herself. "A pony of my very own, can you imagine? One that no-one can take away."

Alice was laying the kitchen table for supper when her dad let himself in the back door. His black raincoat was covered in drops of water and his hair was plastered to his head. He was carrying his briefcase in one hand and a rolled up newspaper in the other. He dropped the briefcase onto the table, shrugged off his coat and handed the newspaper to Alice.

"I picked it up at the station. You're famous. Page five I think it is."

Alice grabbed the newspaper and flicked to the right page. Staring back at her was a photo of Star, taken a couple of days after he'd arrived at Tanglewood, all skin and bone and matted hair. Next to it was the picture of Alice holding Star at the horse show. He looked sleek and polished, the picture of health. The headline read, Rescue pony is a winner.

Alice read the story underneath.

An abandoned pony who was given a second chance by a local animal charity has shown he has winning ways.

Midnight Star was so weak when he was taken in by Tanglewood Farm Animal Rescue Centre that he could hardly stand.

Against the odds, the nine-year-old black gelding pulled through and this weekend took home a trophy at the district horse show.

"Star was a bag of bones when he arrived. In fact we weren't sure he would last the night," said the centre's owner, Julia Hall.

"We have spent the last three months nursing him back to full strength and the results have been amazing. It's incredible to believe that this is the same pony."

Julia said Star's amazing transformation was mainly thanks to the hard work of nine-year-old Alice Winter, who has been a volunteer at the rescue centre since she was five.

Alice rode the pony to victory in the Best Turned

Out class and the pair scooped fourth place in the First Ridden class.

"Alice has spent hours looking after Star and I'm very proud of her. And to win two rosettes at their first show was the icing on the cake," Julia said.

Alice smiled at her mum, who was reading the story over her shoulder, but was surprised to see a look of shock sweep across her face.

"What is it, Mum?" she asked.

"Nothing, sweetheart. Come on, give me that. Supper's ready." She went to take the newspaper but Alice was too quick and read to the end of the article.

Star is now ready to be re-homed and Julia is appealing to families who would like to give the rescue pony a permanent home to contact her.

"No!" Alice cried. "They must have got it wrong. Julia would never let Star go. Tanglewood is his home."

She looked to her mum for confirmation. "Mum? She wouldn't, would she?"

Her mum's face was troubled. "I don't know,

darling. She hasn't mentioned it to me. Maybe the paper made a mistake. Come and sit down. It's time to eat."

Alice shook her head and grabbed the newspaper. "I need to speak to Julia, Mum. I need to find out what's going on."

12

A Life Without Star

Alice dragged herself over the post and rail
fence and headed slowly across the field to the
farm. She felt out of kilter. Numb. Surely Julia
wouldn't send Star away, not when she knew
how it would break Alice's heart? But all the
Tanglewood animals are re-homed in the end,
whispered an unwelcome voice in her ear.
What makes you think Star is any different?

Alice couldn't imagine life without the little
black gelding. If she wasn't by his side she was
thinking about him, planning the adventures
they would have together. In the three
months since he'd arrived at Tanglewood
they'd become inseparable. Star followed her

everywhere, a black shadow at her heels. Losing him would be unbearable. He was the most important thing in her life. There was a lump in her throat the size of a gobstopper, and her eyes felt heavy with unshed tears. She wiped her nose on her sleeve. It was no use crying. She needed to be grown up and matter-of-fact when she made the case for keeping Star, not blubbering like a baby. Lifting her chin, she marched towards the farmyard, rehearsing what to say.

A red sports car was parked at the end of the drive. The car looked familiar, although Alice couldn't place it. Hearing voices in the kitchen, she ducked under the fence and was about to let herself in the back door when she realised where she had seen the car before. In the driveway at Susanna's house. She remembered her friend saying it was her dad's pride and joy. But why would Susanna's dad be visiting Tanglewood?

Alice knew eavesdropping wasn't polite, but she was drawn to the open door like a moth to the beam of a torch. She crouched behind it, her heart thudding, and listened.

"- so when do you think we'll be able to pick him up?" A man's voice. Susanna's dad.

"I need to do a home visit first, but just as a formality. Anyone who's a friend of Alice's is a friend of mine. All being well I should think you can take him at the weekend." Julia's voice was warm. Alice felt as if ice was slowly freezing her insides.

"Susanna is going to be so excited. She's talked about nothing else for days."

"I'm glad. What a perfect ending, after everything he's been through. Anyway, you must excuse me, I have a couple of dozen hungry mouths to feed. I'll give you a ring to arrange the home visit."

Alice heard the shuffle of chairs and leapt to her feet. Julia was suddenly the last person she wanted to see. Not glancing back, she set off for home at a sprint, her mind whirring.

Her mum had finished washing up and was making sandwiches for the morning. "There you are. Your dinner's in the oven. Did you speak to Julia?"

"Not now, Mum." Alice could hear the wobble in her voice. She cleared her throat and tried again. "I think I'll go to bed. I'm pretty tired."

"Alice, what's wrong?"

"Nothing," Alice croaked over her shoulder as she ran up the stairs, two at a time. She slammed her bedroom door and hurled herself onto her bed, pulling the duvet over herself and burying down deep. It was only then that she allowed the tears to slide down her face.

13
Julia's Betrayal

For the second time in a fortnight Alice couldn't eat or sleep. But this time it wasn't nervous excitement that kept her stomach churning and her head buzzing. It was unhappiness. Julia, her second mum, practically part of the family, had betrayed her. There was no other way of looking at it. And as for Susanna...She of all people should know what it was like to have the pony you loved taken from you. Alice couldn't bear to see either of them, and the next morning pretended she had stomach ache so she could stay at home.

"Are you well enough to pop over to Julia's

for half an hour? I promised I'd help her with her accounts," said her mum after lunch.

Alice shook her head.

"Are you sure? Don't you want to see Star?"

Of course she did. She missed him like crazy. If she craned her neck from her bedroom window she could see a corner of his paddock and occasionally she caught a glimpse of him grazing. She hadn't seen him for nearly two days and it felt like the longest two days of her life. She knew she should be spending every spare minute with him, making the most of the time they had left together, but she shook her head again.

"No. You go. I'll stay here."

"Alice, what's wrong? It's more than stomach ache, isn't it?"

Heartache, that's what it is, thought Alice listlessly. But there was nothing her mum could do to make it better.

"Honestly Mum, I'm OK. You go."

Her mum looked at her in concern. Alice hadn't told her what was wrong. But she had pretty good idea. She'd never seen her daughter so upset, even after the accident, when black stitches had crisscrossed her pale cheek like a beginner's attempt at embroidery. She gathered her mobile and keys, her mind made up. As she headed out of the back door, she smiled at Alice.

"This won't take long. But ring if you need anything."

The next morning Alice woke to find her mum sitting on the end of the bed, watching her.

"How are you feeling this morning? OK for school?"

Alice rubbed the sleep out of her eyes and considered the question. She wanted to hide at home forever but knew she'd have to see Susanna sooner or later, and it might as well be today.

"I guess so."

"Good. I thought I'd make pancakes. They'll be ready in ten minutes."

An hour later they were pulling up outside school. Alice heaved her rucksack onto her back, kissed her mum goodbye and made her way across the playground, hoping to avoid

Susanna, who was with a group of girls from their class on the far side of the netball court. But Susanna spied her and ran over.

"Hi Alice, are you feeling better? I missed hanging out with you yesterday."

"Bit better," Alice mumbled, changing direction and heading for the outdoor play equipment. Susanna followed. Alice stopped abruptly and Susanna almost cannoned into her. Alice's face was fierce as she confronted her friend. But Susanna hadn't noticed. She was desperate to share her news.

"How could you?"

"Guess what's happened!" they said in unison.

Susanna blinked. "How could I what?"

"What's happened?" Alice asked dully, although she knew.

Susanna fumbled around in her schoolbag and whipped out her mobile phone. She tapped a few times.

"Look who we're picking up on Saturday," she said, holding the phone out to Alice.

"I already know," Alice answered, pushing it away. "You don't need to rub it in."

Susanna saw the hurt on Alice's face and faltered. "I thought you'd be pleased that he'd found a good home."

"He already has a good home!" Alice cried. "With me," she added in a small voice.

"But you told me all the Tanglewood animals are re-homed in the end. It was only a matter of time. And isn't it better that he's coming to live at my house, where you'll be able to see him whenever you want?" Susanna was upset. She'd had no idea Alice would take the news so badly.

"I've known you wanted him ever since the first day you saw him. But Star's happy at Tanglewood. It's his home." Alice was close to tears.

"Wait a minute. Did you say Star?" said Susanna, her face clearing.

Alice nodded mutely.

"Just look at the photo!" Susanna ordered.

Alice took the phone reluctantly and stared at the screen. The sun was glinting off it, turning it opaque. She cupped her hand over the top and narrowed her eyes.

There was the barn at Tanglewood. Julia was

standing front of it holding a bucket and a lead. Alice held the phone closer so she could get a better look at Star, even though it broke her heart to see him.

But wait a minute, that couldn't be right. She shook her head and looked again. Hope flickered inside her. Susanna took the phone and snapped the case shut.

Alice stared at her, lost for words.

14
The Great Escape

"**B**ut that's Milo," Alice finally spluttered.

"Yes, we're picking him up on Saturday. I thought you'd be pleased."

"I thought...I thought you were taking Star."

Susanna's face was serious. "I remember how I felt when I had to leave Dream. I would never, ever do that to anyone, let alone my best friend."

Alice swallowed. "I'm sorry. It said in the paper that Julia was going to re-home him, and then I saw your dad at Tanglewood. I put two and two together -"

"And came up with about fifty four!" grinned Susanna. "Mum and Dad said we could have a rescue dog so we went to have a look last weekend. We all fell in love with Milo. I didn't tell you in case we failed the home visit. I wanted to wait until we knew for sure. You don't mind, do you?" she asked, her face serious again.

"No, I don't mind," said Alice. "Peter and I are used to the animals being re-homed. I'm glad he's going to be yours. It means we'll still get to see him."

Alice felt dizzy with relief. Susanna wasn't taking Star away from her. And she had described Alice as her best friend. The thought gave Alice a warm, fuzzy feeling.

"What about your new pony?" she asked.

Susanna linked arms with her and they headed towards their classroom. "We're going to look at a couple this weekend. They both sound lovely. I can't wait."

It was only as they sat at their desks and Mrs Johnson had taken the register that Alice realised that just because Susanna wasn't giving Star a home didn't mean that someone else wouldn't. They could be at Tanglewood right this minute, going through the pet adoption process with Julia, while Alice was stuck in the classroom, about to sit a spelling test. She gazed out of the window, a plan forming in her mind.

She had to get out. Now.

Throughout her time at school Alice had always been a model pupil. She handed her homework in on time, she never chatted in class and she was polite and helpful. So when Mrs Johnson saw her sitting at her desk, one hand over her mouth and another in the air, she bustled over to her in concern.

"Everything alright, Alice dear?"

Alice took her hand down and crossed her fingers under the desk. She shook her head. "I'm really sorry, Mrs Johnson. I really don't feel very well."

There was a sound of chairs scraping on the floor as Alice's nearest classmates edged away. Susanna mouthed, "You OK?" Mrs Johnson helped Alice to her feet and escorted her out of the classroom. Soon she was sitting on the scratchy blue sofa outside the school office, a pale pink bucket on her lap and a bundle of hand towels in her fist. Fifteen minutes later her mum pulled up outside the entrance to the school, hurried in and gave her a hug. Twenty minutes after that they were home. Her mum carried her school bag into the house and sat Alice down at the kitchen table and gave her a glass of water.

"How are you feeling?" she asked, feeling Alice's forehead. Her hand felt cool and soothing. "Oh dear, I think you've got a temperature. Try and have a sip of water and we'll get you to bed."

Alice's usually pale face was flushed. It was true that her stomach was churning but she hadn't suddenly come down with a stomach bug. She was ashamed she'd lied to Mrs Johnson, but she'd also felt a rush of adrenalin as her teacher had helped her out of the classroom, and pure exhilaration when they'd accelerated away from school, as if she'd just pulled off a massive diamond heist and her mum was driving the getaway car.

"I'm not ill," she said, pushing the glass of water away. "I needed to see Julia and I couldn't wait until tonight."

"Alice! That's not like you." The shock on

her mum's face made Alice squirm, but she carried on anyway.

"I have to stop Julia re-homing Star. When he came to Tanglewood I promised him he'd never have to leave. He trusts me, Mum. I can't break that promise. Not after everything he's been through. I have to convince her that I'm right."

Alice paused. She eyed her mum, who had sat down next to her. She didn't look cross. In fact she was smiling.

15

New Beginnings

"I wasn't going to tell you until Dad got home, but I may as well tell you now. It'll stop you hot-footing it over to Julia's."

"But -"

"Let me finish, Alice. The thing is, I've watched how close you've become to Star. And I know upset you'd be if he was re-homed. I had a long talk with Dad last night and we made a decision."

The hairs on the back of Alice's neck were standing up and butterflies were leaping about in her stomach. She didn't dare look at her mum. Instead she closed her eyes and crossed her fingers.

"We've decided to adopt Star ourselves. For you. We'll pay Julia for his keep and he'll stay at Tanglewood. It's all agreed. I was signing the paperwork when school phoned to say you were ill." Alice's mum looked at her sternly. "And while I'm on the subject, I don't want you pulling any more tricks like that, Alice Winter."

"Oh Mum!" Alice flung her arms around her mum, tears streaming down her face. "Thank you! I promise I won't. I can't believe it. Star's really mine?"

"Yes, he is," her mum hugged her back. "You work so hard at the rescue centre, we thought you deserved it. And Julia's delighted. She didn't want to see him go, either."

Alice wiggled out of her mum's embrace and grabbed a carrot from the vegetable rack. "Can I go and tell him now?"

"Of course." She looked at the clock. "There's not much point going back to school until after lunch. Stay as long as you like."

Alice let herself out of the back door and ran towards the farm. Her heart was pounding as she jumped over the fence and pelted towards

Star's paddock. The little black gelding was dozing in a sunny spot by the gate. Alice skidded to a halt and watched him for a moment. She couldn't believe it. He was staying at Tanglewood. He was hers and no-one would ever take him away.

As if sensing she was there, he opened one eye and whinnied. She opened the gate and when she walked towards him she felt as though she was walking on air. Star met her halfway, whickering as he found the carrot in her hand. He crunched it noisily and nudged her gently.

She held out her hands. "I haven't got any more carrots. Just some news to tell you." She ran her hand down his neck, delighting in the feel of his silky smooth coat.

"You're staying at Tanglewood Farm, Star. We'll be able to go for rides with Susanna and her new pony and enter lots more shows. We'll always be together. What do you think about that?"

The little black gelding leant his weight back on his near foreleg and took a bow. Alice giggled and curtseyed back.

"My pleasure, Midnight Star. I'm glad you approve."

ABOUT THE AUTHOR

Amanda Wills lives in Kent with her husband Adrian and sons Oliver and Thomas, and their two cats. She spent many years as a journalist and began writing children's fiction in 2013. To find out more about her books visit www.amandawills.co.uk, like The Riverdale Stories on Facebook or follow amandawillsauthor on Instagram.

Made in the USA
San Bernardino, CA
12 May 2020